ACROSS THE BRIDGE OF ICE

Ruth Fox

The Bridges Trilogy
by Ruth Fox
available from Hague Publishing

The City of Silver Light
Across the Bridge of Ice
The Wall Between the Worlds

ACROSS THE BRIDGE OF ICE

The moral rights of Ruth Fox to be identified as the author of this work have been asserted.

This is a work of fiction. All the characters and events portrayed in this book are fictional, and any resemblance to real people or incidents is purely coincidental.

© 2014 and 2020 by Hague Publishing
First Edition (ebook) 2014
Second Edition (paperback) 2020

Hague Publishing
PO Box 451
Bassendean Western Australia 6934
Email: contact@haguepublishing.com
Web: www.haguepublishing.com

ISBN: 978-0-6485714-8-3

Cover Art: Across the Bridge of Ice by Ruth Fox

Typeset Century Schoolbook 12/14

Rarely do you find a book written from the teenage perspective that resonates so well.

Karen Fainges

I loved the beautiful prose, the wonderful descriptions of everything . . . and really loved the story line.

Christina – Ensconced in Lit

An amazing fantasy novel . . . this one will appeal to a large audience; young and not-so-young alike. Highly recommended.

Brenda – Goodreads Top Reviewer

Dedication

This book is dedicated to my parents, my brother, and my husband.

Chapter 1
The Worst Thing in the World

THERE'S a doctor in Outpatients who looks like Count Dracula. Pale skin and black hair pulled back into a bun so tight she can't even blink. I swear all she needs is a black cloak and a pair of bloodstained fangs.

'You need to take things more slowly, Keira,' she says to me every time I go in to see her. I think it's a threat.

See, I'm not a good patient. I'm *im*patient. I find it hard to sit still, which is not good when you've got a broken ankle. Most of the time I'm doing stuff I'm not supposed to, like, you know, *walking*. And . . . well, falling down the front steps.

'I am taking things slowly,' I tell her.

I resist the urge to pick at the neatly folded sheet covering the bed underneath me. Being in this room, with all the neatly arranged equipment and dark furniture, always makes me feel antsy. It probably doesn't help that I haven't slept properly in ages. I keep having dreams about ice. It crackles all over the house, and into the trees, and across the grass and the streets before everything turns white. But as much as I hate seeing doctors, I *definitely* don't want to be sent to a psychologist, so I'll keep those dreams to myself.

'I didn't fall on purpose.'

Mum speaks up. 'I keep telling her she needs to take it easy. But every time I turn my back, she's out of bed making cereal or playing with the dog. And now this . . .'

I feel sorry for my mum. She works long hours running the Cassidy Heights Bakery, and has to be up at four o'clock most mornings. Not to mention the accounts, bills, sales targets, and production quotas she has to meet. Having me home from school has only given her more to worry about.

When a blizzard hit our little suburb of Cassidy Heights two weeks ago, I kind of got lost walking back from my friend Jake's place. I tripped on a kerb and went for a slide on my butt. Yeah, it wasn't exactly my shining moment. Volunteer rescue workers from the State Emergency Service found me eventually, but by the time they called my mum, she was already beyond panic.

The weather system that caused the freak snowstorm has broken up now – according to Channel Seven News and Weather, that is. Of course, there still haven't been any satisfactory explanations about what exactly caused it. I can just picture the meteorologists at the

Weather Bureau scratching their heads. And me, I was kind of planning to get an A+ on my science project about predicting the effects of an arctic winter in a desert country, but I've kind of left my partner, Jake, in the lurch while I'm spending all this time recovering.

'Well, we'll see what these new x-rays show us.' Doctor Dracula waves a sealed yellow envelope. 'Then we'll know whether you'll be able to head back to school. Bet you'll be excited to see your friends again.' She rips open the envelope, tipping a couple of plastic sheets into her hands.

I give her a withering stare. Why do adults assume that school is some fun place where you get to hang out with your friends? It's totally not like that. Teachers spend all their time getting you not to talk, not to sit next to your friends, and not to waste time socialising. I hate school. I hate the rules and regulations.

'All I really want to do is get back to soccer practice.'

'Hm,' says Doctor Dracula. She sticks the x-ray pictures on a lighted board. It's an ominous 'hm', a sound that means *there's something bad here.*

I look at my bones. The inside of people's bodies is pretty interesting. I mean, all those little bits and pieces that join together to make us work. It's kind of fascinating what living beings are made up of.

'What's "hm"?' I ask.

Mum leans forwards, her brow crinkling.

'What we have here is a non-union,' says Doctor Dracula. 'The gap between the broken edges of the bone was a large one, and that fall you took probably pulled it further out of alignment. The bone isn't healing the way it should.'

'What does that mean?' Mum sounds worried.

'Well, we might be looking at an operation. We'd need to insert a bolt to keep the bone in place while it heals.'

'That sounds drastic.' Mum's voice is shaking a little.

'It's a relatively simple procedure, and certainly not uncommon. But I won't lie to you. There can be complications.'

'Complications – like what?' I ask.

'Well, Keira, you may have some pain in that foot for the rest of your life. Also a certain weakness. The bones will never heal as strongly as they were before they were broken.'

'But that won't matter, right? I mean, it's not like I won't be able to walk or anything.' My own voice is shaking a bit now.

'Of course you'll be able to walk. But you may find it difficult or painful to run. You might be restricted in more strenuous activities.'

Slowly, very slowly, it's dawning on me. 'What about soccer?'

She purses her lips. 'We won't rule anything out at this stage, of course. But I'd like to schedule the operation as soon as possible. Mrs

Leichman, we'll need you to fill out some forms . . .'

I don't hear anything else. My mind is ringing with thoughts. What if, what if . . . *what if I can never play soccer again?*

'I'll see you on Thursday, Keira,' says Doctor Dracula.

I nod, resigned, and grab my crutches to follow Mum out of the office.

We get all the way back through the waiting room, through the delay at reception while they sort out some mismatching Medicare numbers, through the slow walk down the disabled ramp at the front door, and the short walk to the car before she starts on me.

'Why don't you ever listen to me? You shouldn't have been moving around. You shouldn't have tried to manage those stairs on your own. If you would just do what you were told for once . . . '

'Don't yell at me!' I shout.

'I don't know how else to get you to listen! You're too stubborn for your own good!'

'I'm the one who might never be able to run again. I think *I'm* the one who should be upset.'

'Oh, really? Wait until you're old enough to be responsible for someone. Then you might understand.'

We drive home in stony silence. I hobble on my crutches through the yard and into my room where I slump on my bed. My door has a busted hinge and doesn't shut properly. I count to three, then sure enough Molly, our dog, noses her way into the room and heaves herself up on my bed. She nuzzles up beside me, her warm body solid and comforting against my side.

'Good girl, Molly,' I whisper automatically, scratching her ears just where she likes it. Her paw twitches in response.

'Keira?' Mum taps at my door. It swings slightly back and forth but she doesn't come in. 'Keira, honey, can I come in?'

'No.'

'I'm going to get some Chinese takeaway for tea. I thought you could invite a friend, if you want.'

It's a peace offering. She knows it's my favourite. But I'm not hungry. 'Alright.'

'It'll be okay, honey,' she calls softly. I hear her footsteps recede to the kitchen, where I know she'll be making a cup of coffee and staring blankly at the wall. It's just been the two of us since Dad left three years ago. We know each other's thoughts like mind-readers.

With a sigh, I roll over and reach for my bag. I pull out my phone and bring up my contacts list. I select the first number on recent calls. It rings once, twice, three times.

'Hello?' says a familiar voice.

'Jake?' I say, then burst into tears.

Chapter 2
The Almost Kiss

JAKE has been my friend since we were in primary school. We ate dog biscuits out of the packet in my garage, sat at the back of the class and punched each other in the shoulder until the teacher wrote our names on the board, and painted each other's hair green in Art. My mum and I were at the hospital on the day his little brother was born. I remember Mum holding Mrs Miles's hand as she was wheeled through the doors into the private room.

Later, when Daniel was older, all three of us spent hours playing hide-and-seek in the pine plantation in Phoenix Park. We built a treehouse in one of the tallest trees of the plantation. You could see the entire world from up there, though the treehouse must be falling to bits by now.

I guess we've drifted apart a bit lately, though. That's what happens when you grow up. I mean, I started going out with Andrew, who didn't really like Jake much. And then there was Baz, and Jake got all awkward about him and me. I wonder if he was jealous. That just makes me feel weird though – I mean Jake is my friend.

Then he met Rebecca, a really pretty, strange, pale girl who stayed with him a couple of days. And he changed. There was something strange about her but Jake never really wanted to talk about her much. I guess he was sorry she only stayed for a few days. Maybe he was really in love with her. And *that* made me feel weird, because I didn't want Jake Miles to be in love with anyone. And what does *that* mean? Is it just because he's my friend and I don't want him to drift further away?

Tonight, he turns up on the porch at eight, and Mum lets him into the lounge room where I'm propped on the couch with pillows and the TV remote, my foot on the coffee table. We eat our Chinese food and Mum goes to bed, leaving us to watch a re-run of *How I Met Your Mother.* Canned laughter echoes from the TV.

'So,' says Jake.

'So,' I reply, picking bits of fried rice off my jumper. 'It's Mikhal's birthday on the weekend. He's having a party on Saturday.'

'You reckon you can –?'

I shoot him one of my best death-glares. 'Of course I can make it. I'm not going to stop *living.*'

'Right, sorry. I was just wondering if your mum would actually let you go. She seems pretty . . . anxious.'

'I told her Mikhal's parents would be there. I also told her I'll just sit on the couch the whole night, because it hurts too much to move anyway. I think she feels bad about the operation, bad enough that she'll let me have a treat beforehand. Besides, I haven't seen Mikhal or any of the others in ages. It's bad for me, psychologically, to be so isolated.'

I bat my eyelids innocently and Jake laughs.

'Cool. Well, I'll ask Dad. I think Nina can drive us. She's been talking to Mikhal's mum a lot, about all this charity stuff – and your mum will be sleeping, won't she?'

I nod. Mum has early nights. 'That'll make things easier. She likes Nina.'

I'm not sure about Nina myself. Every time I see her walking around Jake's house, cooking in the kitchen, cleaning the bathroom, reading in the lounge room, I just picture Mrs Miles, Jake's real mum. Even though it's been years since Mrs Miles died, it just seems wrong to have someone else in her place. For a long time, Jake hated her with a passion, but since the night of the blizzard, he's been warming up to her. I reckon we all got closer that night, so I'm obligated to make an effort to do the same.

'I've gotta go,' Jake says at last. 'I told Dad I'd be home by nine-thirty.'

'Jeez, talk about a curfew.'

'I've got school tomorrow. Or have you forgotten some of us still have to go to class, you lazy bum?'

'I'm not a lazy bum!' I yell, punching him in the arm. He leans over to whack me in the shoulder, but all of a sudden he's too close – his face inches from mine. I can see his lips. I can *taste* his lips. It would take only the slightest movement to kiss him. I could kiss him. For a second it's going to happen. He's going to lean in and kiss me.

My heart is racing. My breath catches in my throat and I pull back – and tumble right off the couch with a yelp.

'Shit!' Jake gasps, catching me in his arms. My breath leaves me. He's strong – strong enough to lift me easily. 'Shit, I'm sorry! Are you okay?'

'Ouch,' I grit my teeth against the pain. My ankle feels like it's on fire.

He lifts me back up to the couch. Something has fallen out of his pocket and digs into my leg.

'What's this?' I pick it up. It's a slender tube made of brass or something heavy. There's thick glass in both ends. It's an old-fashioned telescope. As I touch it, something jumps in me. Like a spark of static electricity, it runs right through me, leaving my hair tingling.

Jake grabs it – I mean, full on snatches it – right out of my hands. 'It's nothing.'

The moment of the almost-kiss is gone. There's no getting it back now. This, whatever this is, has wiped it from existence. 'Why are you carrying around an old telescope?'

'What does that matter?' He tucks the thing back in his pocket, avoiding my eyes. 'Are you okay? Should I get your mum?'

'No. She'll be asleep by now. I'm fine.'

'I'll call you before Saturday,' Jake says quickly, pretty much running out the door.

More laughter blares from the TV. I don't notice anything that happens for the rest of the episode because I'm thinking about Jake. Somehow, he's not just "Miles" anymore. When did I start thinking of him as Jake?

Chapter 3
At Jake's House

I SLEEP the whole night, but as morning comes and I drift towards wakefulness, I hear voices echoing in my ears.

'. . . *uncertain of how this is going to be. The problem lies in the instability of the linkages – there were times when we could predict where a bridge might be . . .*'

The voice is a woman's. It's clear and firm and very, very cold.

'*There were times,*' a man replies, '*when bridges were fixed in place permanently.*'

'*But we must work with what we have.*'

'*There are other ways, devices –*'

'*Hush! Do not speak of such things, not here!*'

There is a long silence and then there's just the sound of receding footsteps. Then Molly's licking my face and I can hear a whistling sound from the kitchen and Mum muttering to herself about matches that won't light.

Sitting home alone today is torture. I keep thinking about what happened the night before, Jake's hands on me, and the almost-but-not-quite kiss.

It's so weird that I'm having trouble believing it. Maybe I made it all up. Finally, I pick up my phone and text him, just to see how he'll respond.

I'm bored!

He replies almost instantly – *you're borING! You suck,* I reply.

He doesn't text back. But later that day, his ID flashes up again.

I have to redo the assignment for science.

I feel a twinge of guilt. It's my fault he failed the assignment. We were supposed to do it together but I landed in hospital, which I guess goes to prove who was the brains behind the operation. And I guess it proves how bored I am when I text back; *do you want me to help?*

His response is neutral. *You don't have to.*

Told you I'm bored, I type. Then I add: *I'll have to redo it anyway when I go back.*

When Mum gets up later I get her to drive me to Jake's house. Jake's dad's car is in the driveway, so she parks on the street. Getting out of the car is such an ordeal I start to wonder if I should have stayed home. I get the feeling we're being watched and, sure enough, when I look towards Jake's neighbour's house, I see that old lady, Mrs Henders, looking out from behind her curtains. She's looking right at me and doesn't even bother to hide it once she knows I've seen her. It gives me a spooky feeling.

Jake's brother Daniel is in the front yard, chucking a tennis ball against the wall of the house.

'Hey,' he says when he sees me.

I grin. Daniel's a good kid. I feel bad when I think about how little I've seen of him over the past year, especially since he hurt himself looking for me on the night of the snowstorm.

'Jake's inside somewhere,' he goes on. 'Does your leg hurt?'

'Yeah,' I tell him. 'What's with your neighbour? She's creepier than ever.'

'Mrs Henders?' he looks across the fence, but shakes his head. 'She's alright.'

'Alright?' When did she become all right? We used to scare each other stupid making up stories about how she ate kids and stray cats.

He shrugs. 'She's just old,' he says. But there's something else in his tone, something he's not telling me. I wrinkle my nose. The whole Miles family is hiding something!

I turn back to Mum and wave, just to let her know I'm okay. She beeps the horn as she takes off. I manage the steps up to the Miles's front door and Daniel thoughtfully opens it for me. I pause inside, looking around.

It's all different now. Someone, probably Nina, has rearranged the furniture in the hall, and the pictures on the walls are in the wrong places. The family photo, the one of Jake and Daniel with their dad and mum, is still on the wall, but there's another one next to it, showing

Nina and Jake's dad sitting in the back of a boat.

Daniel yells out to Jake.

'Daniel! Keep your voice down, will you? Oh, hello, Keira.'

That's his dad, who I can see sitting in the lounge room with a laptop propped next to him –. I remember Jake telling something about him spending more time at home thanks to a promotion. He also told me he's quit smoking, which is probably why he's jiggling a pen anxiously in his hand.

'Hi, Mr Miles,' I say with a smile.

'Your leg . . .' he starts, but thankfully Jake emerges from his room just then, saving me from another explanation of *how things are going*. He motions me into his bedroom and shuts the door.

It's not the first time I've been in Jake's room, but just like everything else since my leg, it *feels* different. He shares the room with Daniel, so there are Transformer toys on the floor, as well as crumpled jeans in the corner, comics on the bookcase, and the smell of Lynx deodorant. Basically, there's twice as much – *boyness* – as usual.

'I thought we should work in here. Nina's cleaning the kitchen. It's best to stay out of the way when that happens.'

He grabs his backpack off his desk chair to make space for me to sit down. He's acting like nothing happened at all.

'So I'm thinking,' he says, fishing through his backpack and pulling out his science book. 'We should stick with our original idea. Well, your idea. About the environment and climate change. It's a good idea. I think we can still get a good grade.'

We scribble ideas for the next half hour. But my mind's not on the task. I'm thinking about my leg, and soccer, and going back to school.

And about kissing Jake.

He refuses to look at me. I can't really look at him either, so I keep glancing around the room. I find I'm staring at Jake's bedside table where there's a little blue bag. There's something inside the bag. A long slender shape. A telescope-sized shape.

'Can you get me a drink?' I interrupt him.

'Oh . . . sure.' He's acting the gracious host, too polite to even crack a joke about me being a slavedriver or something. Damn it, Jake Miles. What happened to you? When did we start being *polite* to each other?

As soon as he's out the door I lunge for the bag and unwrap the object. Yes, it's definitely the telescope. It's heavy and though it doesn't shock me like it did the first time, it seems to vibrate in my hands. It's made of brass, I think, and it's old. Is it an antique? A heirloom? Maybe it's worth something.

I put my eye to the lens and peer at the wall. It's blurry, this close up, and the thick glass puts a rainbow of distorted colours across it.

'What are you doing?'

I whirl around and the excuses I had half-formed in my mind vanish when I realise it's Daniel, not Jake, who's caught me in the act.

'I was just . . .' I stutter.

'You should put that back,' he says.

'I'm sorry. I just wanted to see it.'

His eyes are piercing, accusing. 'So, did you see anything?'

'What am I supposed to see? I just looked at the wall.'

He seems to relax, letting out a little huff of breath. 'It's just . . . you shouldn't touch things that aren't yours.'

'I *know* that. I didn't mean to. I just wanted to see it. You, um, you're not going to tell Jake?'

Daniel flops onto his bed. 'Well, nah. It's just a telescope, anyway.'

Just a telescope? I'm starting to doubt that.

***

Jake and I finish nutting out the project. Later that afternoon I call Mum to come and get me. Jake helps me walk across the yard.

'You! Girl,' calls a voice.

I look over the fence and see the crazy neighbour gazing at me. Mrs Henders has this fixed look in her eyes, like she's trying to see right through me.

'This is Keira, Mrs Henders,' Jake says politely.

'She needs to be careful.'

'Why?' asks Jake. I wonder if he's humouring her.

'There's something . . . I can't be sure . . .' she says. 'Something about her is *changed*.' Then, almost angrily, she shakes her head and stalks away.

I raise my eyebrows at Jake. 'What was *that*?'

He shrugs. 'Sorry. She's okay, most of the time.'

'She's freaking *weird*.'

Mum pulls up at the kerb. Jake opens the car door for me and helps me in, but he still won't *look* at me. And right now, that's all I want!

Chapter 4
The Party

MUM gets a call from Cassidy Heights Hospital the next day. Doctor Dracula has scheduled an appointment for me with a specialist to discuss my operation. I get knots in my stomach, worse than what I usually get before a game. But the meeting is mainly about filling in forms and a lot of explanations about how long it will take my leg to heal, with more *if*'s and *however*'s.

If everything works out, there's a chance I'll be able to regain full movement. *However*, depending on how well the bones knit, there's also a possibility of limited motion. *If* I attend regular physical therapy, I'll be giving myself the best chance. *However*, physio will be hard work and might be very painful.

I stare at the wall. It's covered with certificates, just like Doctor Dracula's walls. All these people have bits of paper saying how smart they are, but none of them can tell me if I'll be able to play soccer next month.

'So, it's scheduled for Thursday. We'll have

to pack your bag again,' Mum says on the way home. 'I got you those new pyjamas –'

'I want to take my old ones. They're more comfortable.'

'You're not taking them. They've got holes in the armpits.'

I roll my eyes. 'No one's going to see my armpits, Mum!'

'I spent good money –' she says, her voice cracks, and I realise she's crying.

'Why are you so upset? I'm the one who's getting sliced and diced!' And suddenly I'm crying, too. I never cry. But even when Mum assures me everything's going to be fine, I can't quite believe it. Right when I need it most, I can't find my usual optimism.

***

Saturday arrives. Despite my protests, Mum sets her alarm so that she can help me get ready. She starts to worry, of course, and almost changes her mind at the last minute. 'I'm not sure it's such a good idea . . .'

But I keep my cool and carefully explain to her all the reasons why it makes sense for me to go. 'One,' I tick this off on my finger. 'The doctors keep saying I need gentle exercise. If I stay home I'll just sit on the couch feeling sorry for myself. Two, I need social activity. It's good for teenagers to interact with one another. We need to keep our minds active. And I'm not going to school, so I'm starting to feel isolated. Three . . .'

I'm struggling now, but if there's one thing I'm good at, it's *talking*. I can talk until the cows come home.

'And three, I promised Mikhal. You always told me it's important to keep your promises. Right? He's my friend.'

The guilt works its magic on her.

She helps me dress. I'm not that big on fashion, so I've had to make a real effort to find something suitable: a mid-length soft denim skirt (practical, given the cast on my ankle), a peach-coloured V-neck top, and a white cardigan. Although most of the ice outside has melted, it's still freezing at night, so I wear a white coat over the top.

Mum brushes my hair.

'You look pretty,' she says.

'You say that like you're surprised,' I grin. But I'm taken aback when I look in the mirror. I'm not used to seeing myself in anything other than jeans or my soccer gear. I look . . . like a *girl*.

Mum spritzes her perfume on me. It's her favourite and smells like violets. I pretend to cough and she laughs.

'Go back to bed.' I tell her. 'Nina will be here in a minute.'

She helps me into the lounge room first and gives me a little black velvet purse with silver patterns on it. I recognise it immediately. She only takes it with her when she goes out to dinner or a movie with her friends.

'Have fun,' she says, and her eyes fill with tears. Oh, great, she's getting all *my little girl is all grown up* on me. You'd think this was the first party I'd ever been to.

***

'Wow, look at this place.'

Jake is standing in the doorway, staring into the nether regions of Mikhal's huge home. The house suffered some damage in the ice storm. One end of the veranda collapsed under the weight of gathered snow, taking several of his mother's prize roses with it. The surviving ones have leaves that are black and shrivelled.

I feel sorry for them, even though they're probably insured for more than my entire house.

'Um, hello?' I remind Jake that while he's busy examining the décor, I'm teetering on my crutches behind him, and I'm cold. The front door has been left open, presumably so people can wander in as they arrive. Inside, the heater is blasting warm air into the entryway.

'Hey!' says Mikhal. He's carrying a packet of chips and a bottle of coke. He pauses when he sees me, his eyes narrowing. 'Keira, you look different.'

That's about as imaginative a compliment as I expect to get from the boys I know.

He leads us through to the lounge room where the TV is on, playing some music video channel. There are already about twenty people here, gathered together in their usual groups. Through the doorway, I can see a dining room table laden with bowls of food and bottles of drink. Some people are in there, loading up on the free sugar.

'Mum was talking to Nina for ages when she called about the party,' he says to Jake. 'She's getting all fired up about charity things. All those people who lost their homes and stuff in the snowstorm, she's fighting some court cases for compensation for them, but she wants to do more.'

'Yeah, I heard.'

'It's her latest thing.' Mikhal rolls his eyes. 'At least it's keeping her occupied . . . means she's not on my back about school.' Mikhal plonks himself down on the lounge and opens his bag of chips, stuffing a handful into his mouth and talking while chewing. 'She hit the roof when she found out Mr Jass failed me on that science project.'

'You and Andrew handed in a GI Joe taped to a boomerang,' Jake points out.

'It was a vital experiment in the effects of gravity and wind vel . . . velo –'

'Velocity?' Jake laughs. 'Maybe next time you should pick a topic you can actually spell.'

'You can talk. You failed too.'

'Are you seriously talking about homework?' I butt in. 'I'm sorry, but you've got all week to do that. Mikhal, how does it feel to be sixteen?'

We talk and laugh. Mikhal convinces Sharna Devon to give up her armchair for me. It's covered in white velour and I feel like I'm dirtying it just by breathing.

Someone turns up the music and dims the lights. The darkness makes the room more comfortable. I'm glad I convinced Mum to let me come. I've missed being around people so much! I've missed talking. But when people get up and start to dance, that's when I feel it. The pain of being left out. I can feel the beat of the music in my feet. I want to be up there, mucking around with my friends. Instead I'm stuck in my white armchair with my crutches stacked next to me.

Something twists in my chest. What if this is it? What if my leg never *does* heal, and for the rest of my life I'll be trapped in a chair, watching while other people move around me?

Fear creeps through me, going deeper and deeper, until it seems like a certainty. I'll never walk again.

I'll never run again.

Someone appears in front of me. 'Hey, Keira.' It's Baz.

He's the last person I want to see at the moment, tears are hovering just behind my eyes. Since we broke up, we haven't talked much. It's a shame because I always liked him. He's usually so easy to talk to because he's so laid-back about everything. Our conversations flowed. We could argue and joke about anything. It was . . . easy.

But after the night of the snowstorm, when everything changed, when *I* changed, I suddenly didn't want 'easy' anymore. I didn't know *what* I wanted. When I broke up with him, I think he was disappointed more than upset. Maybe even embarrassed. He looks so awkward now that I start to feel bad all over again.

'Hey,' I say as cheerfully as I can.

'I . . . um,' he shifts on his feet.

'Don't ask me about my leg,' I growl. 'Don't even mention it.'

He looks shocked.

'I'm kidding!' I laugh, but it's an awkward laugh because I can tell I've made him even more uncomfortable.

'Look,' he manages at last. 'I just wanted to say I'm sorry.'

It's my turn to be shocked. 'What?'

'It's just that . . . you know, when you went missing . . . I should have been the one to notice. To go looking for you.'

He's standing close to me and talking in a low voice. I reach out and touch his hand, and for a moment something really strange happens. It's like – like a window opens in my mind. Suddenly, I'm plunging into a cold rushing river and I can *see* into his memories. I see him sitting in his bedroom, looking out through the window. The snowstorm is raging and I can feel his frustration, his fear and horror at what's happening and at not being able to do anything about it. I can see something dark, like a tiny knot of blackness winding around him. And then I realise what's upsetting him so much. It's that Jake went out to find me. And he didn't.

He thinks he's a coward.

He thinks my leg is his fault.

My fingers move. They pull the knot apart and, as air rushes into my lungs, I come back to myself.

'Keira?' he says, looking at me with concern.

'It's okay,' I breathe.

He seems to know that I'm not just talking about me. 'Is it?' he asks.

'I just said so, didn't I?'

He sighs and, somehow, I see all the worry melt out of him. Inside my mind, it's like the same pure white light from my dreams. He's still awkward, but he's not feeling guilty anymore, and as I let go of his hand, he smiles shakily.

'So, uh, I'll see you around?'

'Sure.' I nod.

I'm relieved when he leaves, but he's just as quickly replaced by Jake, pushing a cup of Mountain Dew into my hands and sitting on the arm of the chair.

'You look bored,' he says.

'I'm not,' I protest. 'I'm just appreciating the atmosphere. I'm going to call it . . . *vibrant.*'

He's wearing a black Killers t-shirt and a brown jacket over jeans. His dark hair is combed neatly. He smells like guy's deodorant and he looks . . . nice.

'Are you okay?' he asks.

Of course I'm *not* okay. You're my best friend and you're keeping secrets from me. I want to kiss you but you don't trust me. You're still in love with Rebecca, who's not even here.

'Fine!' The word comes out too cheerfully. 'I'm fine. Thanks for the drink.'

'You know . . .' he says in a low voice, but at that moment someone steps in front of us. It's Sharna Devon. She's wearing a long green skirt, belted over a loose white shirt. She looks pretty and confident, and she has two legs that work.

'Jake?' she says. 'Hey! Ben ditched me. You want to dance?'

Jake looks taken aback. 'Um – '

'No excuses. You *have* to.' She's grabbing his hands and dragging him away but he's not putting up much of a protest. I watch them weave in between the dancers. Sharna moves easily, her body finding the beat of the music and taking Jake with her. Jake Miles *dancing*? And yet, there he is. And he's not doing too badly.

I wish I was dancing with him.

I shift uncomfortably. Something's digging into my hip. I dig it out. It's a familiar blue pouch. My heart skips a beat. I can't believe it. It must have fallen out of Jake's pocket when he was sitting next to me.

Almost without thinking, I slip the pouch and the telescope it contains into the purse Mum lent me. I glance over my shoulder guiltily but of course he hasn't noticed anything, he's too busy laughing at something Sharna has said.

Chapter 5
The Telescope

THE party starts to wrap up when Mikhal's parents decide the neighbours deserve some sleep. A line of cars run up the wide driveway as parents arrive. Jake comes to find me. He looks troubled.

'So, you can dance,' I say sharply.

'Huh?' Distracted, he furrows his eyebrows.

'You and Sharna. You'd make a good couple.'

He's patting his pockets. I know what he's looking for and I'm biting my tongue, thinking about what's in my purse. But he doesn't notice my discomfort.

'Nina's waiting,' he says miserably, checking his phone.

We head out to the car. Nina asks us if we've had a good time, but neither of us speak for the entire ride home.

***

Later, back in my room with Molly, I pull the

telescope out of Mum's little black bag.

Sitting in my hands, it looks surprisingly *normal* for an object I know is anything but. I only wish I knew exactly what it was!

Molly sits up on her hind legs and rests her front paws on the bed, looking at the telescope, her nose working as she tries to make out its scent.

'What is it?' I ask her. 'Hm? Molly, can you tell me what it is about this stupid thing that made me *steal* it?'

To my surprise, Molly starts to growl. It's a long, low growl deep in her throat. Her eyes are fixed on the telescope.

'What?' I ask her. I reach out to pat her, and suddenly there's a flare of bright white light in my mind. It's like what happened with Baz, but different because instead of actual images it's . . .

Strange-cold-thing, not a thing, not-meant-to-be, not-here, don't-like-this . . .

Thoughts. I'm hearing Molly's thoughts.

What, am I a mind-reader now? If it wasn't so scarily real, I'd laugh at myself. But it's right there, inside my mind. Like a second voice.

Wow. Excitement flickers in my chest. This is the coolest thing! This is amazing! I open my mouth to call for Mum – *'Mum, look what I can do!'* – but I check myself. I can't tell anyone. Who would even believe me?

I don't believe it.

What's happened to me?

Pain suddenly surges in my ankle. I cry out and Molly, startled, dashes out the door. The pain doesn't fade. I grit my teeth and lie down in the bed, pulling the covers over me. I've still got my shoes on. I grab my pillow and hug it tightly, closing my eyes against the pain. But there's no stopping it. It thrums through me in waves. Finally, somehow, I fall asleep exhausted.

Chapter 6
Changing

THE strange dreams come again, full of sharp white ice. It slices my skin whenever I move. Those voices, a woman's and a man's, echo in my ears.

'. . . will be sentenced to time in the cell beneath the Chambers. It's the only solution.'

'I don't like the idea . . .'

'But she's broken the Edict! She needs to be punished.'

'We can't use the –.'

I don't understand what they're talking about.

I wake up a zombie. Mum has the day off and she makes me breakfast. It's a rare treat, usually I'm left to fend for myself. It's hardly gourmet food, just toast and vegemite, but it doesn't taste quite right.

I push my plate away. It's hard to care about food right now. All I can think about is the telescope and what happened last night with Molly. The telescope must have some kind of strange power.

But then ... what happened with Baz? I touched his hand *before* Jake dropped the telescope. And those weird dreams have been happening for ages, ever since I hurt my ankle.

There must be something I'm missing. The best thing to do, the *only* thing to do, would be to ask Jake. But I can't. He'd know I took his telescope if I did that. So once Mum leaves for work, I hobble back to my room feeling as if the telescope is calling to me.

I pick it up and run my fingers over its surface. I examine the imperfect circles of glass in both ends. I put my eye to it and aim it at the walls. I run it over the ceiling. I peer at my desk and the bits of lint on the carpet. I turn to the window.

And I gasp.

I'm looking at the sky above the hedge between our neighbour's house and ours, and I'm seeing something that's impossible. There are buildings and towers stretching up like the delicate pale fingers of angels, linked by a cobweb of bridges as fine as lace. I can't believe it. It's an entire city hanging in the sky.

I lower the telescope and blink my eyes rapidly.

Nope. It's definitely gone but ... I know it's still there. And, somehow, it seems perfectly natural for it to be there.

Something inside me tingles. The sensation runs down through my injured leg and pools in my ankle, prickling the skin.

There's something else . . . the buildings . . . I've seen them up-close. I've stood beneath them, climbed their stairs, walked through their cavernous rooms. It's almost like . . . I can remember what it's like to be there.

In the city.

The white light from my dreams, it's not white at all. It's *silver*.

***

I become aware of the clock on my bedside table. The red numbers tell me it's 7:31 pm. That can't be right. I've only been here . . . an hour, surely? My stomach rumbles uncomfortably, confirming the clock's readout. It *is* late. I've missed lunch. It's almost dinner time.

But I don't care. The city . . .

I see the telescope on my lap and realise my hands are cramped from holding it. I'm not surprised. If I've really been lying on my bed and looking through the window at those beautiful spires for five hours . . .

The city!

I look through the telescope again. The city is still there, shining a little more brightly now in the afternoon light. It must look incredible at night . . .

I pull myself away. I can't let it take me again. I have to . . .

What was I going to do? Oh, yes. Food.

I grab my phone and scroll down to Jake's number. He should be out of class by now but there's no answer when I call. *Damn it!* I have to speak to him. I have to ask him about the city and . . .

What am I thinking? I can't ask him. He'll know I've got his telescope and then I'll . . .

I can't think!

'Hello?'

It takes me a moment to realise that there's a voice coming from my phone. They've been trying to talk to me while I was spacing out. But it's not Jake's voice.

'Who is this?' I ask.

'Daniel. Jake left his phone in his bag. I just grabbed it.'

'It's Keira,' I say. 'Can you get Jake?'

'Yeah, I know who it is.' Of course he does, my number is in Jake's phone, he'd have seen who it was when he picked up. Duh.

'He's not here,' Daniel is saying. 'He went over to some mate's place.'

'Who? Maybe I can call him there.'

'Mikhal, I think.' He sounds suspicious. 'He was in a hurry. He . . . um, left something behind last night. Lost it.' His voice is slow, as if he's thinking about something he doesn't really want to say.

'Okay, I'll try Mikhal's –'

But Daniel leaps in. 'Keira? You know, about the . . . about Jake's telescope . . .?'

My heart leaps into my mouth. *He knows.*

They all know. You're a thief, you'll lose the telescope, they'll take it back —

'You were looking at it the other day. I'm just wondering. You didn't . . .'

'Didn't what?' My voice is shaking. I'm shaking. *Stay calm and breathe,* I tell myself. *He hasn't said anything yet.* 'What about it? It's just an old telescope, right?'

'Right!' says Daniel, with relief in his voice. 'Anyway, Jake lost it. I just wondered if you'd seen it, that's all. You were at the party, too, weren't you? You didn't see if he dropped it?'

'No. I mean, if I had I would have given it to him. It's an heirloom or something, right? He probably shouldn't have taken it with him.'

Stop talking, Keira. You'll give yourself away.

'No, he shouldn't have.' Daniel's voice sounds like a kid's when they think someone older should have listened to their advice. 'It's just that it's pretty special, and . . . should I tell him you called?'

'No.'

It's okay – nobody knows. I'm safe.

I shake my head. 'No, actually, don't tell him. He'll see if he checks his phone. Thanks, Daniel.'

'That's okay.'

I hang up, feeling shaky. That was close. I have to be more careful. I have to try and think straight.

From Daniel's voice, I know for sure that *he* knows what the telescope is. Whatever secret

Jake is keeping, he's let Daniel in on it. And Daniel is just as worried about it being losing it as Jake. Suddenly, I'm angry about being excluded. I've got as much right to know this as they do, don't I? Why am I being kept in the dark? Why doesn't Jake trust *me*?

I mean, he's gone from being Miles to being Jake in *my* mind. And it was only a few days ago that we *almost* kissed. So I've got a right to be trusted, don't I?

I mean – look at what's happening to me. Whatever it is, I know it's all got to do with that city in the sky.

So why can't I *know*?

These thoughts sprout branches and roots, playing over and over in my mind, until all I can think is that if he's not going to tell me his secret, he deserves this. And I'm glad I stole the telescope.

Chapter 7
The Bridge

'KEIRA?'

Mum knocks on my door, and I quickly shove the telescope under my pillow.

'Yeah?' I call.

'Keira, a friend is here to see you.' Mum pushes the door open and I see her looking a little confused. Standing behind her, peering around her arm, is Daniel.

'Daniel?' I say, surprised. 'Um, hi. Is Jake with you?'

'Nah,' Daniel says. 'I just . . . I um . . .' he looks really nervous, almost anxious. I try to remember the last time he came to my house. It would have been over a year ago, and only ever with Jake.

Then Molly jumps off my bed and noses him happily to show she remembers him and Daniel crouches down to pat her.

'I'm going to start dinner,' Mum says. 'I can take you home afterwards, okay, Daniel?'

Daniel nods and Mum vanishes, leaving us alone.

'What's up?' I ask Daniel.

'Well,' he says. He's scratching Molly behind her ears, but his eyes are looking over my room, searching for something. 'I was just . . . wondering . . .'

'What?' I'm defensive. I shift so that I'm hiding my pillow from his view. There's only one thing he could be here for, and I'm not going to give it to him.

'Did you take Jake's telescope?' He blurts this out in a rush, his face turning red. 'I'm not mad or anything. Jake won't mind. I won't even tell him. I didn't tell him about you looking at it, so I'll keep this secret too. But you have to give it back.'

Daniel's voice is urgent, pleading. He's smart for his age, but right now he sounds like the nine-year-old kid he really is. I kind of feel like I owe him, really, for missing out when he went from being Jake's little tag-along brother to an actual person.

But I can't let that guilt get to me. I look him in the eyes and lie.

'Sorry.' I manage a regretful sigh. 'I really don't know anything about it. I wish I could help you find it.'

Daniel's face goes a darker shade, but this time there's hot anger behind the redness.

'Yes you do. You're lying. I know you took it.'

'No, you don't,' I counter, just as angrily. Why is he accusing me? Even though he's right, I feel an intense rage about the fact that he suspects me. It's stupid and irrational, but I can't stop it building inside me.

'And I didn't. If Jake lost it, it's his fault! It's got nothing to do with me.'

'You have to give it back!' Daniel's voice rises. He's almost shouting now. Molly backs away, alarmed. 'You can't keep it. It's . . . it's special. And dangerous.'

'Dangerous?! How can a telescope be dangerous? What's so special about it?' I challenge him, daring him to tell me, to reveal the secret. 'What does it do?'

'I . . . can't . . . tell . . . you!' His hands are clenched at his sides. He almost looks like he's going to start tearing through my possessions and that worries me. There's nothing I could do to stop him except shout for Mum, and that would only cause more awkward questions.

'Just give it back. It's not yours.'

I feel strange. My own fists are clenched on the bedspread, and they feel cold and rigid. When I look down, I see white frost speckling the floral coverlet around my fingers. It crackles and little wisps of cold mist curl upwards.

'What . . .?' Daniel begins, but at that moment Mum appears. Obviously, she's heard the yelling and I quickly draw the bedspread up to hide the ice crystals.

She turns her concerned gaze on Daniel. 'Is everything all right?'

'Yes,' Daniel replies. 'I think I'll . . . I'll just go home, now.'

'Do you want me to drive you?' Mum offers, but Daniel is down the hallway and through the front door before she finishes her question.

'It's fine, Mum,' I say, suddenly feeling really tired. 'He thought I had something of Jake's. I don't.'

Mum doesn't look convinced, but she decides to drop it. 'Well, dinner is ready. You could use a good meal. I don't like how pale you are.'

Dinner is macaroni cheese. I'm not a big fan of this at the best of times, but tonight it tastes like salt and mould.

'Are you all right?' she asks me. 'You look like you're coming down with something.'

'I'm fine,' I say, but I'm not sure how convincing I am, given I can't keep my attention on anything for longer than two minutes straight. Not to mention the food, which is churning in my stomach.

'Do we have any lettuce?' I ask.

'Lettuce?' Mum furrows her brow. 'I don't think so. What's wrong with your dinner?'

'Nothing,' I tell her sulkily. I feel bad, Mum put a lot of effort into making this, but I can't eat it. It's all wrong.

'I think you should have an early night,' Mum decides. Even though it's only 8:00 pm, I don't argue with her. Once I'm settled under the covers, with Molly snuggled in next to me, I pull out the telescope.

Just as I imagined, the city is even more amazing at night.

It's made of silver and light. Of my *dreams*. And it's *mine*. My city.

'Look at that, Molly,' I whisper, burying my hand in her fur. The pulse of her heartbeat leaps under my fingers.

Happy, friend. Content. Wonder . . . food?

I smile at her simple thoughts, the way she can find pleasure so easily.

Friend.

'If only my problems were so easily solved.' I say. 'But I don't even know where to start.'

Friend . . . scent . . . not . . . changed-somehow-odd

Suddenly Molly whines. The tone of her thoughts is altered. The soft, malleable ease is disrupted, like someone's thrown a stone in a pond and disturbed a perfect reflection. She sits up and looks at me reproachfully, then leaps from the bed.

'What's wrong, girl?' I ask her. She whines again.

Cold. Cold cold cold. Friend? What's happening? Changing?

'Molly?'

But she trots through the partly open door, leaving me.

I point the telescope back to the city and I see the change that has spooked Molly so badly. There is a bridge out there.

A bright, glittering bridge stretching from the road up to the sky. The arch is so gentle, so delicate, that it looks perfectly natural. As if it's always been there and I've only just noticed it.

I press my hand to my head. I feel cold, as if I've got the opposite of a fever. I turn on my bed lamp and realise my skin is pale, almost blue. Little beads glitter on my fingernails.

Frost. Ice.

If I was that cold, I should have hypothermia. I should be shivering. I should be *dying*!

But I don't even *feel* cold . . .

'Mum?' The whimper escapes my mouth before I can stop it. It doesn't matter, she wouldn't have heard my quiet voice, but I clamp a crackling hand over my mouth anyway. I can't call Mum! She'll freak out. It'll give her a heart attack.

I grab my phone.

I hit the redial button.

Jake answers almost immediately. 'Keira? Is Daniel there? He said –'

I cut him off. 'There's a bridge, Jake.'

'A what?'

'I can see a bridge to the city through the telescope. Don't pretend you don't know what I'm talking about. I can see it. I can see it right outside my window.'

'Keira! Whatever you do –'

'No,' I interject once more. 'No. You don't get to tell me what to do. You should have told me!'

'Look, Keira, I'm sorry. I'll come over right now and explain.'

'Explain what? The ringing in my ears? The

way I can hear my dog's thoughts? The weird freakin' dreams? I'd like to hear that explanation, Jake! I really would.'

'Don't do anything. Just stay where you are. I'll come . . .'

His voice continues but I'm no longer listening.

My crutches are propped against the bedside table. I grab them and manoeuvre myself out of bed. I hardly feel the pain in my leg but the tingling is overwhelming. It's running through my entire body. I feel like I'm going to explode.

I swing my way through the door. The floorboards creak as I hobble-hop to the front door, but there's no sign of movement from the lounge room. I see Mum asleep on the lounge.

Even if she'd been awake, I don't think she could have stopped me. The need to be outside is so great, I can't think about anything else. Vaguely, I'm aware that I'm still holding my phone. I can hear Jake's voice coming through the speakers. It's tinny and distant.

Cold air surrounds me. I cross the veranda and ice crackles along the boards. Just like in my dream!

The bridge is so close. It's made out of that pure silver light. It doesn't look solid but I know, somehow, that it's designed to be this way. It's made of something stronger and more durable than anything man-made. It's narrow, barely wider than a footpath, tilting and slanting in places like a piece of curling ribbon on a gift.

It looks like ice, but it's not. It's something from another world. It gives a bit under my feet and my crutches. I step carefully. There's nothing to stop me going over the edge if I slip.

'Keira!'

I can still hear Jake's voice coming through the speaker of my phone but it doesn't seem real. Looking through the blinding light of the bridge, nothing in my world seems real anymore. It's like it's on TV, a computer-generated image, something someone dreamed up to fill in the background.

Step . . . swing . . . step.

'Keira!'

It's not Jake's voice, not this time. It's higher, clearer but just as urgent. I start to turn around to see who it belongs to, but halfway through the movement I forget why I'm looking back. The bridge is ahead of me. I have to get to the bridge.

Step . . .

'Keira . . . come back . . . it's –'

Step . . . swing . . . step.

Someone grabs my arm. I pull free. Looking down, I see a small hand, dark against my pale skin.

'Daniel?' I say, or I think I do. Sound is doing strange things here. The whiteness is so bright, and I can smell something . . . it's sweet, sharp and tangy . . .

'What are you doing here? I thought you'd gone home.'

I can only catch snatches of his words. 'I came back . . . knew you . . . lying . . . *please come back . . .*'

I laugh. 'No, I'm not going back.' *Not . . . back . . .* my own voice is being torn away from me.

He shouts 'You have to! You'll wreck the balance!'

And then, there's the smell of burning.

The silver light surrounds me, draws me in. I'm part of it now, part of the light. It's so easy to move. I feel almost weightless. The pain in my leg is nothing but a distant memory. My body, my stupid, useless body, seems to travel easily through this space.

It's right. It's perfect.

I don't look over the edge. I don't want to see Cassidy Heights, my city, my world. I look straight ahead.

The city of silver light reaches down for me with welcoming arms. It lifts me up into its streets. Its buildings surround me. The dazzling light fades, leaving me standing in the centre of a paved courtyard.

There is a fountain in the centre, a crystal-clear arch of water spouting up and over a beautifully carved piece of stone. Neatly trimmed ice-white grass surrounds it. Trees with pale bark stand in the corners, their roots covered by soft purple-grey moss. Tiny star-shaped flowers hang from the bricks of the walls which rise up on each side.

I'm looking at a small girl who has just emerged from an open doorway in the wall. She wears a short cream-coloured dress with a blue sash and is staring straight at me with horror and amazement.

'Um –' I extend a hand to her. I mean for the gesture to be friendly, but it's the wrong thing to do. She shrieks and backs away.

I realise that I'm burning. There is fire all around me. I can't feel the heat. *That's strange.* And then it hits me. It's like I've run straight into a solid brick wall and I crumple to the ground.

'Keira! Keira!' It's Jake's voice coming through the phone.

Then I hear Daniel, panicky and anxious, from somewhere over my shoulder. 'Keira! Where are you? What's happened?'

'Daniel?' I try to call, but my mouth doesn't work. I clutch the cold cobblestones like an anchor. My stomach roils and I dry retch. Everything inside me clenches.

Inside my head, the girl's shout of fear echoes loudly. 'Demons!'

Chapter 8
From the Below World

SOMEONE is speaking.

'I'm not sure it's a good idea –'

'There are so many other factors. What if she's carrying disease, or some type of bacteria from the Below World–'

'She doesn't look ill, apart from the damage to her leg.'

'The Guardians *must* be informed.'

Whoever's speaking, they sound concerned. I'm drifting, knowing I need to wake up, but I have no idea how to drag myself out of this murky, sticky cloud of sleep.

The voices continue and I hear strange words, like a foreign language, but it's one I've never heard before.

'*Hylifar I najulid,*' one voice says. 'If we don't . . . oh, Archon! You know they'll find out. If Arina felt the disturbance, you know the others will. It won't be long before the monitors at the Etherium track it here. We can't afford to have that happen!'

'I *know* all that, Sarinne.' This second voice

sounds constrained, stiff, as if the speaker is trying, very hard to stay calm. 'You don't need to keep reminding me.'

There's a pause, then he continues. 'But you know what will happen to her if we turn her in.'

The voices fade as if they're moving away from me, and my mind drifts. It's like slowly coming up from underwater. I realise that something is wrong. This isn't one of my dreams. I'm lying on something soft. My head seems to be tilted back, and I'm looking up at . . . what?

Rocks?

It looks almost like quartz, faintly transparent, geometric forms protruding and receding. I've seen photos of cave ceilings like this. But when I turn my head, I can see this is a room, not a cave. There are a few pieces of furniture made out of something dark, like wood, but with the texture of metal: a table with a vase of those star-shaped flowers in it, a shelf holding a jug and a folded white towel, chair with a rounded back, and a long, low bed on the other side of the room. The bed is made from the same material as the chair and there is someone lying in it, flat on their back and perfectly still.

For a second my heart freezes. Is that other person dead? Is this a morgue? Am . . . am I dead?

The walls themselves are semi-transparent and almost glow, as though lit from behind. I can see straight through the one in front of me. There are two people but, through the crystal-like partition, they're only shadows.

'– asking me to do this.' This voice, from the one named Sarinne, is clipped and angry. 'I'm not going to –'

'Are you awake?'

Startled, I twist onto my side and, while the movement makes my head spin, I see a pair of bright blue eyes staring into mine. It's her, the girl I saw in the courtyard. The one who called me a demon.

She's holding my mobile phone in her hands. It's open and she hits a button, causing the screen to light up. The familiar dull glow shocks me. The way the light falls on her hands and flickers over her hair . . . it's proof I'm not dreaming. I'm not dead. This isn't a morgue. I *did* cross the bridge.

Where am I?

'What is this?' the girl asks.

I open my mouth but my tongue doesn't co-operate. All I can manage is a garbled 'Uh.' I reach for the phone and she pulls it away. I try again, but I can't reach her. My arms refuse to obey me and I fall back onto the bed. The stuff underneath me gives a little, feeling soft and squishy, like an air mattress.

'It's a demon-stone, isn't it?' the girl says. She looks about the same age as Daniel, but she speaks as if she's much older.

I work my tongue against the roof of my

mouth, building up saliva so I can form the words I need. 'It's mine,' I croak. 'Give it back.'

'No!' she says stubbornly. 'It's pretty, and I like the sounds it makes. I want to hear the voice again. I'm going to keep it in case it does.'

'What –' I start to ask her, but suddenly the phone disappears from view as she slips it into a pocket of the cream-coloured dress she's wearing. She looks towards the partition with a guilty expression as both figures step into plain view. One is a woman; it must be Sarinne. She's tall and wearing a long grey robe belted at the waist with a beaded sash. She has straight silver hair and a narrow face. Her skin is ice-pale, her eyes clear blue. The other is a boy – or a young man wearing a similar robe but with a hood. A few strands of yellowish hair poke out from underneath. His face is a bit more rounded than the woman's, his nose slightly crooked, and there's a hazel tint to his eyes. He looks more . . . *substantial*.

'Arina!' says Sarinne sharply. 'You shouldn't be in here alone. It's not safe, *pirrisi*.'

'I heard her cry out!' The girl protests. 'I wanted to make sure she was alright. My Teacher says a Healer should always be vigilant.'

'Arina, you haven't earned your Second Level sash yet.' Sarinne says this gently, but she sounds a little anxious, as if she's not quite sure whether she's saying the right thing. 'It would have been better if you'd at least spoken with me before coming in here.'

'Yes, Mother.' Though it's not a very convincing apology, Sarinne doesn't seem to notice. Her attention is distracted by me. She bends down to peer into my eyes.

Arina peers over her shoulder at me. 'Is it a demon?'

'Near enough to one,' Sarinne says.

Behind her, the young man's face clouds with anger. 'You cannot say that! She's done nothing wrong. Not to mention –'

Sarinne turns away from me, silencing him with a glare. '*That* has nothing to do with *this*,' she snaps, gesturing, making it clear that the '*this*' is me.

'You're not supposed to talk about him!' Arina sings, but Sarinne turns to her and frowns.

'Arina, you have studies to attend to, do you not?'

With a reproachful glance at her mother, Arina leaves. When she's gone, I breathe a bit easier. I don't know what it is about that girl, but she makes my skin crawl.

'I'm not a demon,' I say. It seems important to get that cleared up straight away.

'We know that,' says the young man. 'We know exactly who, and what, you are.' His gaze is curious, inquisitive. Obviously, who and what I am is very interesting, to him at least. 'But there are still . . . questions.'

'I've got a few questions, too!' I nearly explode with the words. 'What's wrong with me? Why can't I move? I can't feel my leg . . . and how do you know who I am? How can you?'

Ignoring me, he moves closer, but he's still wary. 'How did you come to be in our garden?'

'I . . . I don't know,' I answer honestly. 'I was . . . I walked . . . across the *bridge –*'

'A bridge?' he gasps. 'You crossed a bridge . . . into our garden?' His eyes shine with something, both disbelief and hope, I think. 'But there was nothing there when I went out, after Arina shouted. It must have already collapsed.'

'Wait, what?' I yelp. Again, I try to struggle upright, but I don't get far. 'It's gone? But . . . but I –'

The bridge. I have to get back to the bridge. It can't be gone. It was real and solid. I walked across it. It can't just be *gone*!

Sarinne looks as if she's had her worst fears confirmed. 'If there was a bridge leading from our garden, the Guardians will think we had something to do with it.'

Archon shakes his head. 'They have no proof. We could . . . we could hide them.'

Sarinne raises a pale eyebrow and laughs incredulously.

'Hide them? Archon, you know better than that! The Guardians have been watching for anything unusual since the crossing. You've said it yourself, the Institute has noticed an increase in the ruptures and cracks, an agitation in the flow of the *vinarhi* . . . all since the tainted one returned.'

'Of course I know. I tried to find out more –' he pauses, noticing the look on Sarinne's face, and sighs. 'Mother! Don't worry so much! I was careful but I didn't find anything. No one knows what happened at the trial.'

'Then see sense, *hirtharbri*! That is exactly why we must inform the Guardians immediately,' says Sarinne. 'Before the balance is disturbed any further.'

I've been looking back and forth between them as they talk over my head, like I'm at a tennis match.

'What are you talking about? What do you mean?' I plead. They both look at me and, behind Sarinne's stony expression, I can see she's torn. She quickly looks away. She doesn't answer me and shakes her head at the young man.

'Oh, Archon. You and your damned obsession. Why can't you let it go? Why can't you let *him* go?'

When Archon replies, his voice is soft. 'How can I? Mother, how can *you?*'

There is a long silence.

'Hey!' I say finally. 'Can you please –?'

But Sarinne takes Archon's arm, pulling him away. They're gone, and I'm left alone.

Chapter 9
Archon

I DRIFT into sleep.

I'm walking through crystal-lined passage-ways and through rooms that look like my bedroom. My mum stands at one end of a narrow bridge.

'Keira? Are you there?' she calls, but when I try to call back to her my mouth refuses to work.

'. . . scarce moments ago, a report of some kind of disturbance. The cause isn't known.'

'This is not acceptable. Why the delay?'

'The reverberations are so widespread they're acting like echoes. Pinpointing the actual source takes time.'

'Then we will have to begin sooner than I thought.'

It's the same woman I've heard in my dreams. I can see her, almost. She's tall, thin, and wearing one of those long robes with a red sash. I think I've known all along that she's one of them, a city-dweller, before I even knew there *was* a city.

*'There have been other reports of disturb-
ances. If it continues, they might even make the
first move.'*

I wake up breathless and sweaty.

The room is empty, except for the other bed,
and the person lying in it.

For a moment my mind refuses to work then,
suddenly, a panicked thought grips me. 'Daniel?'

I try to sit up and manage to get halfway but
it's an effort. My muscles aren't tired or weak
but something is holding me down, pressing me
back against the soft surface of the bed. It's
easier to lie back and give in.

But it *is* Daniel lying on the far side of the
room, I can see his spiky brownish-blonde hair
against the ice-rock walls. He's dressed in a
short grey smock like a hospital gown and he
doesn't move.

'Daniel?' I call again. 'Daniel! Wake up.'

The figure stirs and moans. 'Wha –'

I'm so relieved to hear his voice, I feel tears
prick my eyes. 'Daniel! We crossed the bridge.
Are you all right? Are you hurt?'

'I can't move.' His voice is high-pitched. He's
scared and trying not to freak out. I've got to
give him points for courage.

'It's okay, it's okay!' I tell him. 'I can't either.
They've done something to us.'

'Who? What did they do? I can't even move
my toes!'

'It's some kind of magic spell or something,' I
tell him. 'And they, well, I don't really know

who they are. What they are. Or *where* we are.'

'Shar,' says Daniel. His voice is suddenly quiet and he stops struggling, as if he's just realised something. 'We're in Shar.'

'The city, right?' I ask him. 'The city in the sky. We're actually there?' How is this possible?

'Yeah,' says Daniel. 'It's the silver light city. We're there.' I strain once more against the invisible force holding me in place. If it's true, and we're in this Shar city, I want to be able to move. I want to see it. I *don't* want to be flat on my back. It's too much like being trapped in that snowstorm with my ankle blazing with pain, unable to move and just *waiting* for someone to come to help me. I can't stand it.

I hear footsteps and the young man, Archon, walks into the room. He's still wearing a hooded tunic, and this time I notice a purple sash around his shoulder and waist. Seeing me struggling, he purses his lips.

'You shouldn't try to move,' he rebukes me gently. 'Sarinne has set a mild restraining aura around both of you. Only for your own safety,' he quickly clarifies. 'You're injured, and I'm not sure how to treat your wounds. I'm not used to dealing with your . . . biological makeup.'

'Biological makeup?' I ask slowly. 'What do you mean? What's so weird about my biology? I'm just a normal person.'

'It's because we're from Earth,' Daniel says. 'That's why we're different, isn't it?'

Archon looks strangely delighted at this

admission. Maybe there's something wrong with *him*, not me. He might be insane. And I'm stuck here, trapped at his mercy . . .

He nods. 'Yes. Your bone density, your blood type, even the placement of your internal organs is . . .' his tone is too reasonable, too thoughtful, for him to be a nutcase. I hope. 'Fascinating, utterly fascinating.'

'So you're what,' I ask, 'a doctor?'

'I'm a scientist,' he says proudly. 'An Etherologist.'

'What's that?' Daniel asks.

'I study the movements of particles between the worlds,' he says, only too glad to answer the question.

Archon pushes back his hood and, for the first time, I see him properly. He's even younger than I thought. In fact, I don't think he's any older than I am. His hair is a sandy colour and it curls around his ears, looking a little unruly. His eyes are a light brown rather than hazel, like chocolate. He looks nothing like Sarinne, even though he called her mother. He looks even less like Arina, who must be his little sister.

A scientist? But he's just a kid.

Daniel voices my thoughts. 'You're really a scientist?'

'Shouldn't you still be in school?' I add.

He furrows his brow, as if he doesn't quite understand why we're questioning him.

'I am. That is, I am still undertaking instruction from my Teacher. But in two weeks, I reach the age of majority.' He looks at me. 'Why are you asking me this?'

I laugh. 'Are you serious? No one our age is a scientist.'

He stands up straight and puffs out his chest. I've seen guys do this thinking it makes them look bigger and tougher, usually before I kick their arses in soccer training. Archon's chest is pretty scrawny, and it's clear I've insulted him.

'When I take the exam, I'll be inducted into my guild and I'll be given First Level Access to the Libraries and Archives. I'll be able to broaden my research, and with my findings about both of *you* –'

Findings? About *me*? About *us?* It's frustrating that I can't move because I want to punch him. 'We're not lab specimens!' I tell him. 'We're human beings.'

'Exactly!' he beams. 'That's what makes you both so amazing.'

I don't know why, but I feel a wash of embarrassment. I don't want him scrutinising me like this, not when I can't move.

He continues, oblivious. 'What I really want to know is, how did you find a bridge? They're so rare. It's very hard to predict where one is going to form. Even the most skilled Etherologists are often wrong.'

My spinning head is starting to ache. 'I don't know. I didn't mean to come here. I didn't even know what the bridge *was*. It's like I was drawn to it. Like I didn't even have a choice. I had to cross it.'

'You were just walking towards it,' says Daniel. 'Like you were sleepwalking. You wouldn't stop, even when I called you.'

I remember. 'I couldn't stop,' I correct him. 'Even if I'd wanted to.'

Archon furrows his brow. 'That is interesting.'

'What's interesting?' I question him. 'Do you know why this happened to me?'

'Not exactly, no. But I have an idea.' He turns and moves a few paces away, then turns back. He holds his hands out, palm up, then moves them up and down as if creating a scale.

'There is a balance of powers and forces between your world and mine. The balance shifts to accommodate fluctuations and . . .'

Seeing my expression, he falters. 'I'm sorry. I can see you don't understand.'

'No!' I reply. 'No, I don't understand at all!'

Taking a deep breath, he continues. 'Let me put it this way. There are causes, and there are effects of those causes. When one power is disrupted, the others must follow, and so we have –' here he waves his hands towards the walls of the room, including whatever it was beyond them as well 'life, the universe, everything we know.'

'That's what I tried to tell you,' Daniel declares triumphantly. 'There's a balance. You can't cross over without something bad happening.'

'Not necessarily,' Archon says, 'I think that if

you were drawn to one of the bridges as you say you were, then this is part of that balance working to bring things into alignment. The *vinarhi* would have been exerting its force over you.'

I think I'm starting to see what he's getting at. 'So basically, I'm here because I was supposed to come here?'

'Possibly. What I'm really saying is that there was a hole in the barrier, and something was forced inside to mend it. It seems that something was you. Does that make sense to you?'

'No,' I say, although it sort of does – as long as I don't think about it too much. 'What about Daniel? He wasn't drawn here like I was. Like he said, he was trying to stop me from crossing the bridge.'

Archon turns away from me to examine Daniel quizzically. 'If he came with you, it can only be because he has some part to play, also.'

'But if we're meant to be here, does that mean we can't . . . can't –' I almost choke on the words, 'go back? I heard you talking. You said the bridge we crossed was gone.'

Archon looks uncomfortable at this and his eyes flit across the room and back. I think he's afraid of how we'll react to his answer, and that tells me all I need to know.

He doesn't think we can go home.

When he speaks, his tone is measured. 'In the past, the bridges were more stable than they are now, and the people of our worlds could use them whenever they chose to. But that was in ancient times. Now bridges appear and disappear randomly, and it seems to be getting worse. No one can predict when and where they will form. Sometimes they last for months, and sometimes they vanish in seconds. You might be able to use one of them . . .'

That doesn't sound comforting. We could spend the rest of our lives here waiting for a bridge to be found. Not to mention, if the bridges are as unpredictable as he said, what would happen if it suddenly vanished beneath us while were crossing it.

Daniel gasps suddenly. 'But . . . the telescope!'

My heart skips a beat. Of course! How did I forget that? 'Yes! That's what showed me the bridge in the first place. But . . . does it even work from this side?'

'We have to try it!' he says urgently. 'Where is it? You've still got it, right?'

I strain to look around the room, but I can barely move my head. The girl, Arina, has my phone. But I don't know what happened to the telescope. Did I drop it in the garden? I try to think back to the first few minutes when I had first stepped off the bridge. Nothing. The wonder of seeing this world blocked out everything else. Then there was Arina calling me a demon, the fire, and . . . me falling over.

'Don't strain yourself!' Archon cautions, just

stopping short of actually pushing me back onto the bed. 'What are you talking about?'

'Was there anything in the garden when I came through? It looks like a long tube, made of metal?'

He looks thoughtful. 'No, there was nothing there when I arrived. Arina found you first and called for Mother. I only came afterwards, when I heard the commotion. I found two long sticks lying next to you. But I didn't see anything like what you're describing.'

So he'd found my crutches with me. But what about the telescope? What if I'd dropped it on the bridge? I can't believe I was so careless. Despair washes over me.

'You mean it's lost?' Daniel's tone rises in pitch. 'Keira! I told you it was valuable!'

'I didn't do it on purpose!' I snap. 'I didn't do any of this on purpose.'

'Whatever it is,' Archon says. 'We will sort it out. I promise you.' His expression is pained, as if he knows how much it means to us.

'How can we? We're stuck here, in this place, strapped to beds and you're going to examine us or whatever –' I stop myself there. Daniel is listening. I can't let him see how worried I am. I need to be positive.

Archon sighs and looks apologetic. 'I'm sorry you're being kept here like this, both of you, but I promise I'm not going to hurt you.' He looks between us and his face is kind, slight regretful. 'I've been remiss.'

He moves out of my vision and I hear the sound of water pouring. He returns with a cup.

'I'm not thirsty.'

That's not true. Now that I think about it, my throat is incredibly dry. But something in my mind is ringing alarm bells, some distant memory about eating the food in fairyland and being trapped there forever.

'I promise you, this is only a restorative tea. Please drink it. It will help you.'

'I don't need it. I'm fine.'

'I swear, I won't harm you.' Archon holds out the cup, sounding like he's trying to coax a scared cat. I catch his eyes and something in them makes me believe him.

If what Sarinne said is true, I'm too valuable to him as a source of information about my world. And I'm so thirsty it's driving me nuts. But it's not just that. I know, somehow, that I can trust him. I let him pour the liquid into my mouth. It's cool, soothing and tastes a bit like gingerbread. After two days of not being able to taste anything properly, I feel like I'm drinking pure heaven.

'My name is Archon,' he offers.

I nod, even though I already knew that, and decide I can give him mine.

'Keira. And this is Daniel.'

Archon pours another cup, crossing to Daniel's bed, but he looks back at me.

'You have no idea how glad I am to meet you both. Welcome. Welcome to Shar.'

Chapter 10
Prisoner

WHATEVER is in that drink, it works wonders. I feel calm and collected. Suddenly, everything seems fine. I'm buzzing with energy. I'll find the bridge and we'll both go home. My leg will heal. I'll go back to soccer. I'll get picked up by a talent scout and I'll be playing pro in no time. This will all be a distant memory.

Archon leaves us. When he's gone, I turn my head as much as the invisible restraints will allow.

'I'm sorry,' I say to Daniel. 'If it wasn't in the garden I don't know where it is.'

If I expected him to forgive me, I would have been disappointed. But I don't. I know this is my fault. I just wish there was a way I could fix it.

But I don't know how to do that, either.

Neither of us says anything for a long time.

I sleep, and when I wake up again, it's dark. Well, dark*er*. The rock walls seem to have dulled, the inner light muted. I guess this means it's late evening although there is no real night in this world.

How can I know that?

I try to push myself up. The restraint is still there, like some sort of invisible forcefield out of Star Trek. I can't push through it. I groan in frustration. I feel like if I could just pull it aside, I'd be free, but there's nothing *to* pull.

Or is there?

Nothing I can see but I can feel it. It's like a heavy blanket covering me, pulling me back down. Instinct tells me to close my eyes, since they're not helping me anyway, and once I do, I can feel it more clearly. Just like what happened with Molly, and in the kitchen with Mum, the sensation of everything around me becoming a thousand times clearer. There *is* something covering me. I pluck the corners of it with my fingers. I can undo the knots that are keeping it there. It's simple, easy. I can feel the loops and links. I slip my fingers in between and flick them aside.

I open my eyes.

The restraint isn't entirely gone. It's like pushing through something thick and gooey, but I manage to sit up. I move my legs gingerly, but, amazingly, there is no pain in my injured ankle. In fact, I can't feel anything at all.

I realise I'm wearing a long grey smock, just like Daniel's, tied at waist. I'm not wearing anything underneath. *Oh, brilliant!* It's only slightly better than a hospital gown and I've had enough of those to last me a lifetime.

'Daniel?' I whisper. But he's asleep, and he looks peaceful. I decide not to wake him.

A knot of guilt forms in my stomach. Why did he have to run out after me like that? What was he doing out there, why didn't he go home when he left my house? It's one thing for me to be trapped here but Daniel? I have to get him out of here.

I look around for my crutches, but they're nowhere to be seen.

Dizziness washes over me. But I have to get up. I have to find that telescope! How will I get home without it? I heave my heavy body away from the bed, and see that it's just like Daniels', a long shelf made out of the duller metal/wood stuff, and the soft mattress on top is like quilt stuffing.

I take a step, but my leg doesn't take my weight at all.

'Ah!' I yelp, as I just manage to grab the edge of the bed and haul myself back onto it. The wrong way round. I'm flat on my stomach, but I don't care. Blackness creeps in at the edges of my vision.

'Dammit!'

Daniel wakes at my yell. 'Keira? Keira, are you okay? Hey! Hey!' he shouts loudly. 'Someone help!'

I groan. Even though the pain is gone, the injury is still there. And I might have just made things a whole lot worse I think grimly, as I feel myself sliding towards blackness.

***

'. . . have to call them immediately. There's nothing for it. She needs a Healer.'

'Then let Arina look at her!'

'I don't want your sister near her, Archon. You should know better –'

'Please! I do not think she has harmed herself. It was a just a mishap. If you call the Guardians, Sarinne, you know she will face the same fate as that tainted girl you took to the cells.'

An impatient sigh, more harshly whispered words, and she's gone. Archon marches over to my bed and sees that I'm awake.

'That was foolish,' he hisses. 'I told you about the restraint. You should have listened to me.'

'And you should have listened to me.' I'm mad, frustrated, and scared about my leg. I'm also worried they're never going to let us get out of these beds, so I think up a lie.

'I had to go to the toilet. You people still do that in this world, right? Or is it just something we *humans* do?'

He blushes. Good. I'm glad I've embarrassed him.

'You should have called for someone.'

'So I'm a prisoner?'

He looks shocked. 'No! You're . . .' he pauses here, unable to deny it.

'How did you do it?' he asks instead, his voice quiet. 'How did you remove the restraining aura? Sarinne works in the lower levels of the Chambers, in the cells, and knows what she's doing when it comes to restraints. You shouldn't have been able to get out of the bed at all.'

'I don't know!' I say truthfully. 'Why does it matter? Can't you at least get me my crutches so I can walk around this room? And maybe you could let me use the bathroom. Even prisoners get to have a shower!'

'You want . . .' he seems confused. 'Crutches, these are the sticks you had with you in the garden?'

'Yes! They help me walk.'

He looks like he's trying to hold back a laugh. 'They're such primitive things! But I can't allow Arina in here to apply a motion charm. Sarinne would not be happy if I let her near you again. I suppose they'll have to do.'

Archon leaves the room. I look across at Daniel, who is blinking sleepily. 'You want a shower?' I ask him, trying to make it sound like a normal, everyday question.

He makes a face. 'I want to get out of this bed,' he answers in a way that tells me exactly how fond he is of showers.

Archon returns at that moment, carrying my crutches. I guess they're no match for a motion charm, whatever *that* is, but I'll deal with it.

'Daniel needs a wash, too,' I say. Archon looks dubious. 'Come on. I promise we won't run away or cause any problems.' I even add the word 'please', which is not something I do very often.

Archon looks unsure, but then he gestures with his fingers and Daniel is released. Daniel sits bolt upright, relief visible on his face. 'How did you do that?' he demands.

'It is difficult to explain,' Archon says. 'To understand, you need to be able to work the Ether which humans cannot do.'

'Ether?' Daniel asks. 'What's that?'

Archon shakes his head. 'There will be time for explanations later. First, you should come with me.'

Chapter 11
Silver World

ARCHON leads us around the partition and into a long hallway.

'Move slowly,' he cautions.

I'm just glad to be moving at all. Moving without pain from my ankle is such a luxury. It's so easy! I haven't been able to do that since . . .

My confidence is short-lived. One of my crutches twists under my weight. Off-balance, I put my hand out to the wall to steady myself while I get my crutches back underneath me. The surface is cool and slightly rough under my fingers. It's solid, but brittle. I can feel ridges where small cracks run through. It's formed in sections, I realise. But then, I already knew that, didn't I?

'You *grow* the walls,' I say in wonder.

'Grow them? You mean, like crystals?' Daniel chirps excitedly. 'We grew crystals at school last term.'

'Yeah, we did it in science class as well,' I say. 'It was with some chemical, alum, I think, and boiling water in jars. Mine never grew. I was . . .' I stop, embarrassed. I'd missed some of the instructions because Andrew and I had been passing notes to each other behind his propped-up science folder. I'd been giggling because he was being so silly, and because I knew people were watching us.

I hadn't known anything about a silver city in the sky then.

'Anyway, I think I mixed too much in, or not enough . . . so when everyone had these pretty crystals growing on a string, I just had . . . a string.'

'The way you describe it is . . . wrong,' Archon replies. 'Rock-crystals are not just . . . *things*. Our homes are built in harmony, not with force. We grow them, coax and train them.'

'Like pets?' Daniel says.

Archon turns his head to one side, confused.

'Pets,' I explain, balancing my crutches so I can use one hand to pat the air, as if I'm stroking Molly's back. 'They're tame animals you keep in your home. I have a dog at home called Molly. She's gorgeous. Don't you have any pets?'

Archon shudders. 'No. They are something of the Below World. I've read about them. And they are one of the things we are warned about by the Teachers. They are dangerous, are they not? They're not capable of rational thought and they can turn vicious. They spread dirt and disease. We have nothing like that in Shar.'

'Really?' Daniel asks. 'But animals are awe-some. Damien's got a parrot called Jack that even talks. It says "Hungry Jack's hungry!" And it whistles to the theme song of *The Simpsons*.'

Archon's expression shows his revulsion. 'Animals are primal beasts. They shouldn't be allowed to live among civilised beings.'

I think about Molly. Gentle, loving Molly with her big shining eyes. She wouldn't hurt a fly. But there are dogs who turn vicious, aren't there? You hear of dogs mauling little kids, and stingrays killing grown men. Animals *can* spread disease. Look at the black plague. And, well, even Molly is sometimes . . . less than clean.

Daniel continues. 'What about insects? You have to have insects, right?'

Archon motions that we should keep moveing down the hallway. 'We have bacteria. Microbes. Small parasites, as well. But nothing large enough to become a pet. However, the essence of your argument is right. The crystals are like pets that need to be looked after.'

There are several doors in the hallway, most of them simple openings without doors, some covered by thin curtains of some kind of net-like material. I catch glimpses of desks and tables as I hobble along on my crutches. There are chairs and shelves made of that strange half-metal, half-wood material, intricately carved; brightly designed carpets on the floor, patterned rugs of swirling shades; and hangings on the walls of woven, shimmery threads that change colour as I pass.

The house is beautifully made. Everything is in its place. There is no clutter, no mess, no books or clothes on the floor, no scattered shoes or discarded newspapers. But there's something missing. It's as if things are slightly wrong. Even Mikhal's huge mansion has the feeling of being *lived-in*. This house feels unnaturally clean and ordered. Like someone had gone through and carefully erased any sign of personality.

As we pass a hall-stand, Archon reaches out to straighten the flowers in a tall colourless vase. Seeing me watching, he explains: 'We are due for an inspection soon.'

'An inspection? Like at camp?' Daniel's inquisitiveness earns him a sharp look from Archon, who is probably getting fed up with the constant questioning.

'I don't know what "camp" is, but it's important that our house is kept in order. We have to impress the Guardians.' Archon seems keen to cut this explanation short, and before I can ask him more, he points to a doorway that leads to the left. 'Here, these are the bathing rooms.'

This room, thankfully, has one of those thin curtains across the doorway. It's not large, and it's not furnished with anything other than a small set of shelves holding folded cloths by the door. Instead, pillars of the rock-crystal slice randomly from floor to ceiling, and I catch reflected snatches of my distorted silhouette. There is a small cubicle sectioned off at the rear. In the middle of the room is a sunken pool, ringed with steps cut into the floor. Water runs into it through a narrow channel, trickling through an outlet in the wall. It swirls around the pool before disappearing through a grate on the other side. The pool is divided into three sections by large sheets of opaque rock-crystal, like cubicles in an office, so that more than one person can use it at once and still maintain their privacy.

'Here are some fresh robes,' Archon says, retrieving a bundle of clothing from the shelves near the door. The robes are a pale grey colour, which I know means they're to be worn by those who aren't affiliated to any of the Guilds. The sashes are neutral as well. I'm more excited about the undergarments, though: I never thought I'd be so glad to see a singlet and underpants. He adds some towels to the pile in my arms. 'And bath-cloths for you to dry yourself.'

'No bath bombs?' I quip, but he stares at me blankly.

'Well,' I continue, 'Maybe some privacy would be good.'

He blushes and backs away. 'Of course. I'm sorry.'

Once he's vanished, I can't help laughing.

'Will you be okay, getting in and out?' Daniel asks.

'I'll manage,' I say. The thought of getting clean is very appealing. I feel sticky and stiff with dried sweat. But I wish I had someone there to help me when Daniel crosses behind one of the other sections and I balance myself against the pillars, putting my crutches to one side and peel my clothes over my head. Lowering myself into the pool is a painful, awkward process.

The water, though, is totally worth it. It's clean, clear and fresh, not too warm and not too cold, and it feels like silk against my skin.

'What is this stuff?' Daniel's voice echoes from the other side of the room.

It doesn't feel quite like water. It's thicker, like milk, but lighter, like fog. '*Vinarhi,*' I say. 'It's called *vinarhi.*'

'What?' Daniel says. 'How do you know that?'

'I don't know.' I didn't want to tell him about my dreams and admitting that I don't know, well, that's not a lie, exactly. 'I just do.'

'It smells clean.'

'Violets,' I tell him. 'It smells like violets.'

But it doesn't, not really. It smells sharp like freshly-cut grass and sweet like summer storms. It smells like everything I've ever smelled, and yet, nothing like them at the same time. I remember reading once that human brains can only process things in terms that are familiar to them. If they experience something strange or unusual, they have to compare it to something they've already seen, heard or *smelled* before. So that's exactly what I do.

Violets, I tell myself. *The vinarhi smells like violets.*

I duck my head and scrub my hair. When I come up, I call out to Daniel.

'Daniel? Why did you follow me? I thought you'd gone home.'

'Don't be mad,' he says after a short pause. 'I was really angry at you. I knew you had the telescope. I didn't want to go home without it. I didn't want to have to tell Jake I thought it was you who took it, either. So I walked around a bit, then I realised I had to go back. I had to make you give it back somehow. I was going to . . . well, I don't really know. But when I got to your house, you came out, and everything . . . happened.'

I press my lips together. 'You should have gone home.'

Silence.

'Daniel, I'm really sorry. If I hadn't stolen the telescope . . . and lied about it . . . you wouldn't have –'

'But Archon said we were meant to be here. If you hadn't stolen it, something else might have happened so we'd end up here anyway.'

I'm surprised by the fact that he's not screaming at me, blaming me for stranding us here. I wish I could be as accepting as he is. By the time I drag myself out of the water, I'm feeling amazing. I dry myself and wrap my hair up, pulling on the undergarments – the singlet is fitted, and kind of doubles as a bra – and belting the new robe with the sash. Despite the strangeness of them, these are the most comfortable clothes I've ever worn.

I lift myself with my crutches and head for the commode. Once I'm done in there, I run my fingers through my hair and I can hardly believe it. For the first time in my entire life, it doesn't feel tangled. It falls easily into ringlets. I peer at my reflection in the pillars. And when I see myself, I let out a little scream.

'Keira!' Daniel yells. 'Are you okay?'

I turn my head from side to side.

No. I'm not okay. This can't be me. I'm pale. Really pale, like a ghost. My hair is tinged with silver, and the curls are limp. My freckles have all but vanished. My face looks thin. And–

'My eyes!'

Daniel's reflection appears over my shoulder. He looks solid and dark next to me. Like I'm stealing all the light from him and leaving him in shadow.

Those are *not* my eyes.

They're blue.

'I didn't want to say anything,' Daniel says quietly. 'But that's how I knew you took the telescope. You're starting to look like . . .'

I've seen eyes like that before.

'Like what?' I ask him.

'Like . . . like . . .' he stutters, then unable to say it, he scampers out of the room, leaving me there with the reflection that's not me.

I look . . . neat. Straight and even. I'm amazed, and scared, but I . . . I like it.

When I emerge from the bathroom, I feel like a new person.

Daniel and Archon are waiting a little bit further down the hallway, sitting on a pillowed seat set into an alcove. Archon glances up, staring at me with wide eyes. Feeling uncomfortable, I shift on my feet.

'You look . . . well,' he says.

'It's amazing what a bit of water will do, right?' I laugh. I'm not a self-conscious person, and never have been. Most of the time I go around in jeans or my soccer gear. Girls like Sharna Devon spend ages in the toilets at school, fixing their hair and makeup. The most time I've ever spent looking at myself was probably two seconds ago in the bathroom.

But now, standing in front of Archon with my hair brushed and my grey hospital smock replaced with the soft robe, I'm very aware of what I look like. I wonder if he thinks I'm pretty.

Before I can wonder about it much more, Archon stands abruptly. 'I need to take you back to your room.'

As we walk, Daniel can't seem to help himself and his normal inquisitive nature bubbles to the surface. 'Where does the water in the pool come from?' he asks.

'All the water in our buildings are channelled from the waterfalls,' Archon replies. Actually, I think he's kind of enjoying telling Daniel about Shar. 'But it isn't *water*, not as you know it in the Below World. It . . . perhaps I should show you.'

He motions to his left, and leads us around a corner in the corridor.

Somehow, with all those windowless walls surrounding us, I hadn't truly realised that there was an entire city out here. But one side of the hallway is lined with open windows, and I'm confronted instantly with the city. It spreads out around us, below us, above us; towering, sparkling, elegant buildings, archways, bridges, walkways.

'Wow,' Daniel gasps.

I can't even manage that much. My mouth hangs open as I manoeuvre closer to the windows.

Below, I can see multiple levels. Terraces give way to winding stairs. Arches support long, meandering paths. There are tall white trees with pointed needle-leaves growing beside them.

And the people! Some of them are so distant they look like specks, but a path passes just metres away, and I watch a woman carrying a white bag walk briskly towards a man, a hand raised in greeting.

I crane my head to look up.

The sky, overhead, is a brilliant, deep blue. It looks like night, the stars are out, and beyond them are hundreds of distant golden lights. It's weird but I can pick out the shapes of countries I know. The bridge I crossed didn't just lead straight here, like the bridge from one bank of a river to the other side. Somehow it went around everything and distorted everything I've ever been taught about how space works. But it's Earth, up there – my home.

Even though it seems to be night-time, it's not dark in the streets of Shar. Everything is lit by the beautiful silver glow that comes from the water.

'The waterfalls,' Archon explains. 'We call it water, although there is another name for it – *vinarhi*.'

Daniel looks at me, as if he wants to ask how I could have known that.

'It means 'source',' I murmur.

'How did you know that?' Archon asks, looking puzzled, but I look away. I'm not telling him about my dreams, either.

Source. It's a strange word, since the water doesn't seem to *have* a source. It's just . . . there. A tumbling flood of whiteness that doesn't look like water at all, just like . . . light. A river of light. It rushes through the city, curving around the bases of the buildings. Some of the water arches over and through the walls; running through apertures and channels and creating hundreds of miniature waterfalls as it spills back out to join the main channels.

'It's beautiful,' I say, hoping to avoid further questioning as I lean forwards on my crutches to look over the scene below.

The design of each building is different.

Some are made of glass, or whatever passes for glass here. Others look like stone, polished smooth and inlaid with different coloured tiles. The roofs are domed or arched; a few are even turreted like old castles.

'Were all of these buildings grown?' Daniel asks.

Archon nods.

'That's the Etherium,' he says, pointing to one of the turreted buildings which resembles a fairytale palace. 'That's where I work, on the second floor in the office of records.'

'Down there is a *huliadra*,' he points to a wide street lined with more buildings of different sizes. 'It's . . . a shopping precinct, a marketplace. And beyond that, just there, are the Chambers.'

He indicates a group of five spires, linked by delicate arches to a towering central pillar. You can tell they're important buildings and they look like they've been there forever; like they've been *created*, not just *built*.

I gape at this spectacular sight. I know exactly what it feels like to walk beneath the walls of that place. I can remember the coldness of the stone emanating from the walls. The long curving steps. The echoing hallways. The carefully manicured gardens. I've seen it all in my dreams.

'The Chambers are the headquarters of the Guardians. They contain the law courts, council rooms, the Hall of Records, the Central Healers Hall and, in the lower levels, the cells.'

'You have a jail?' Daniel says, surprised.

I know what he means. It's hard to imagine that criminals would exist in this place.

'I remember you said something about a prisoner that your mother, Sarinne, was dealing with.' I say.

He nods. 'Sarinne works with the prisoners in the cells deep under the main building. It is an awful place.' He shudders in a way that makes me think he's seen this place up-close, and what he saw there had terrified him.

'Only a few people commit crimes that are bad enough to warrant imprisonment, and most people who are imprisoned apply for *valatha*. Sarinne makes the arrangements when they do, and organises the processes and records afterwards.'

'*Valatha*?' I ask. This is a word I haven't heard in my dreams. I'm not sure I want to know what it means.

'Yes. It's unusual for a person to resign before they reach old age, but if they feel true remorse, it's allowed. Even encouraged . . . and it is a harmonious resolution, so it serves the balance.'

I have a feeling that by 'resigning', he doesn't mean quitting a job. But before I can ask, Archon turns back to the view, eager to talk about something else.

'Over there is the library and the archives. I spend a lot of time reading there, and researching. There are smaller libraries further away,

which I go to when I can . . . they have some
have fascinating ancient scrolls and texts.
Some people are lucky enough to have private
collections but, although I've applied for access,
most of them reject me.'

'You have books? I would have thought you'd
be all high-tech. With computers and stuff, you
know?'

His eyes light up. 'Computers? What do you
know about computers?'

I shrug. 'Everyone knows about computers.
They pretty much run our world.'

'Can you tell me?' He's like a puppy with
those pleading eyes. Just like Molly when you
pull out a box of biscuits and she stares at you
with her tongue hanging out, hoping she'll get
one.

'I've read about them but the information is
highly protected, and what I have read has
been censored by the Guardians. I'd love to
know more.'

I move away from the window, where Daniel
is craning his neck to look up at the lights of
our world.

'I don't really know much. I'm into soccer,
not IT . . .' I can see Archon doesn't understand
what I'm saying. 'Soccer. It's a sport. We get
into teams . . . and we sort of play a game with
a ball . . .'

He smiles. 'Oh, I've heard mention of such
things,' he speaks in a lowered voice, as if he's
afraid we'll be overheard. 'We have nothing like

that in the city. We don't . . . encourage competition. We are taught to achieve as much as we can for ourselves. But outright competition isn't encouraged. It's one of the things the Guardians fear most about your world, the way you place importance on such things; the value you place on violence and rivalry.'

'But sport isn't like that! It's a game. It's about pushing yourself to do your best. That's what winning is about. You make it sound like we bash each other over the head with clubs or something.' I frown. 'Hold on, if knowing about stuff like that is illegal, how did you find out about it?'

Archon looks away, slightly guilty. 'I read a text,' he says distantly. 'It was an account written by a . . . a traveller from your world. But it was confiscated before I could complete reading it.'

'What's confiscated mean?' Daniel asks, pushing away from the window.

'It's when someone takes something away. Like –'

'Like when the teachers confiscated my scooter, right?' Daniel asks. 'But why would the Guardians take away your book?'

Archon raises his eyebrows. 'Because of the Edict, of course,' his voice sounds firmer. 'Documents like the ones I read are strictly regulated. They can't allow just anyone to access dangerous knowledge.'

'Why is it a bad thing to have information?' I

ask. I know I sound like Daniel, but I need these answers. 'Don't you have a right to know something if you want to?'

'What if it was information on how to ruin a crop? Or how to build a weapon that could destroy an entire building? Or the quickest way to kill a person? Your world is full of secrets like that. That's why the Guardians enforce the Edict. It controls the information the public can access. It's a good thing, everyone knows that.'

'But . . . you must be annoyed if it holds back your research. Why should they know stuff about computers if you're not allowed to?'

'Well, I –' he looks a bit flustered, and I can sense he's not telling me everything. Sarinne had been lecturing him for disobeying the rules before and I think he's done it more than once and probably been caught for it.

'It's not just information about computers,' he says, trying to explain. 'They keep track of information about all the technology that has caused so much crime, war and misery in your world. If knowledge on how to build a gun fell into the wrong hands, it could devastate Shar.'

He looks me squarely in the eyes and, for a moment, I'm struck breathless. He's really . . . *hot.* Not in the way swimsuit models are. He doesn't have chiselled features or rippling muscles. He doesn't even have Jake's casual good looks. If he was in our world, he'd be one of those men you could almost call beautiful, without it sounding like an insult.

'Keira,' he says, jarring my thoughts back to the present. His tone is serious. 'This is why you have to be careful. Both of you. When the Guardians find out about you . . . I'm not sure what their reaction will be.'

My heart starts to race. I don't like the sound of this. 'Don't tell them we're here, then.'

'You don't understand. It's not possible to keep you a secret. They will know you're here.'

'How? Nobody knows about us except you and Sarinne. And your sister.'

He shakes his head. 'I told you about my life task. Etherologists work for the Guardians, monitoring the *vinarhi*; if there's a fluctuation, or a disturbance, they have to report it. They might have done so already. The resounding echoes will be noticed by the Etherium. Keeping you here is a risk, especially since our household is already closely monitored.'

'What can they do, though? They're not going to hang you or anything, are they?' I gulp. 'Or us?'

'I'm . . . I don't know, Keira. I don't know exactly what they will do.'

'Oh, great!' I laugh incredulously. 'That's reassuring.'

'Keira?' says Daniel, and suddenly I realise that he's been listening closely. Daniel's a smart kid. He might not understand every word, even I don't understand exactly what Archon is saying, but he understands enough and he looks very worried. 'If we were meant to come here, why would they want to hurt us?'

Archon looks unhappy. 'They are very scared of your world. And I've been in trouble before, that's why we're scheduled for routine inspections by the Overseers. This time, my position at the Etherium may be in jeopardy. There will be . . . repercussions.'

'Then why are you doing this? Is it really worth it?' I ask.

He sighs. 'You are a mystery, Keira. What is happening to you isn't something I've ever seen before. In truth, all I've wanted to do is to talk to you. To be able to say I had spoken to a true human being is something I've only dreamed of.'

I manage a weak smile. 'Well, I hope it's been worth it.'

'It has,' he says, and I can tell he means it.

Chapter 12
The Change

ARCHON motions down the hallway, and we walk on. Well, the others walk. I hobble. I watch the changing view from the windows, and try to contain my amazement at the sight of those towering buildings, the winding streets, the layers upon layers of this beautiful city.

'Why are you so fascinated by the world of humans, when you've got all this?' I ask Archon.

'Yeah,' Daniel adds. 'Compared to Shar, Earth is kind of . . . lame.'

Archon ducks his head as he shows us back into our room. He's suddenly hesitant and I wonder if he's about to reveal what it is he's been hiding from us. 'I suppose it's because of who my father was. It is seen as . . . . a reason to be ashamed, among my people –'

'They're not supposed to be out of bed!'

I recognise that voice. It's the girl, that little *pest* of a girl. She's standing by the wall, her arms crossed and an ugly expression on her face.

'I was simply showing them the house, Novice Arina,' Archon says warily. 'No harm will come to her.'

'I'll tell Mother,' she insists. 'It's dangerous to let them out of the sickroom. There's a risk to her wound if she's moving around.'

'Novice Arina, I promise you, I took care to be gentle,' Archon reassures her, but he looks nervous.

I can't believe he's taking this kind of attitude from a kid! I would have been smacked if I'd spoken like that when I was her age. But the girl doesn't seem to realise how she's behaving. Her eyes move from me to Daniel and back again.

Daniel steps forwards, and holds out his hand as if expecting her to shake it. 'I'm Daniel,' he says. It's an overly polite gesture for someone so young to use, but it doesn't look out of place coming from him. Daniel is the type of kid who would offer to help old ladies across the road.

But Arina recoils from him. 'Don't touch me,' she hisses. 'I know it's a trick! You're a demon! You're trying to spread some disease or parasite from your dirty world.'

Daniel chews on his lower lip. I'm not sure whether he's stung by her comment or trying not to laugh. 'Why would we do that? We're not demons, no matter what the Guardians tell you. We're pretty much just like you.'

'What would you know about us?' Arina fires

back. 'Most people on your world don't even know Shar exists!'

But Daniel did know, I think. Somehow, he knew about all of this.

'You don't belong here,' she continues. 'I won't let you pollute Shar.'

She whirls on her heel and dashes out of the room. Archon looks defeated. I feel sorry for him having to deal with a younger sister who acts like she's head of the household – and gets away with it.

'How can you let her talk like that? She's what, ten years old?'

Archon sighs. 'She is young, but she's a Novice Healer. She works in the Healers Hall in the Chambers. It's a position that commands respect.'

'How can she have a job already?' I ask. 'She can't be any older than Daniel. On Earth, you'd both still be in school.'

'I wish *I* could get a job,' Daniel says, his face serious. 'I would be a fighter pilot. Or a vet.'

Archon looks like he wanted to ask Daniel what a vet is, but then collects himself.

'Our life tasks are determined when we are young,' he tells me. 'If a Sharian shows aptitude for one particular area, they are given special training. Arina is younger than me in years, but she will be able to take her Second Level exam soon, just as I will.'

I think about this. Arina definitely seems older than a normal ten-year-old. If time really does pass differently here, maybe children mature earlier . . .

'You should get back in bed,' Archon suggests. 'Before she comes back.'

I nod, and hop towards the bed, putting a hand on the spongy surface to steady myself.

The skin of my hand looks like tissue paper when you hold it up to the light. I stare at it for a moment, alarmed. Archon notices my horrified gaze and I see sympathy in his eyes.

'What's happening to me?' I whisper.

Archon's expression is miserable. 'I can't answer you, Keira, because I don't know. It might be the effect of being here in Shar but you were like this when we found you. I think the changes have been going on for longer.'

Of course they have. The ice I'd found on my hands and face. Hearing Molly's thoughts. They all happened before I came across the bridge. But . . . there's more. I've felt strange, different, since I broke my ankle that night of the blizzard.

I see my reflection looking back at me from the crystal walls. I want to brush it away, make it melt or disappear the way my dreams do. But it doesn't. It feels cold and solid under my touch. It won't let me pretend this isn't happening.

'What will happen if it keeps going?'

I know he doesn't know, and his silence confirms it.

'Don't worry, Keira,' Daniel says. He's parroting my own words of comfort back at me. I said the same thing when he woke up in that bed, unable to move. It doesn't help at all.

My stomach roils and my vision blurs a little. *It's okay*, I tell myself. *Just breathe.* 'I think I need to lie back down.'

'You're not going to put a spell on us again, are you?' Daniel asks

Archon looks regretful. 'I have to,' he says. 'I'm sorry.'

Daniel makes a little sound, a whimper, but he lies down obediently.

I have trouble getting back into my bed though. I lean my crutches against the wall and try to lift my legs but start to slide sideways. Before I slide far though Archon catches me. His touch zaps through me like lightning and I gasp. This time it's a thousand times stronger than what I felt when I touched Molly. I see . . .

Books, hundreds and thousands of them. They're piled high on shelves carved from the same quartz-like substance as the walls of this room. I long to touch them, to know what's written on their pages. It burns me.

I see a woman. It's his mother, Sarinne. She looks livid, but also frightened. *'Archon! What are you doing?'* she hisses angrily. *'If you're caught, you'll be tried. The Guardians show no leniency to those who break the Edict. Why do you risk it?'*

'You know why!' he answers earnestly. 'I need to know. I have to know where he came from! I want to know <u>him</u>.'

'I'll have to go to the Guardians,' she says. She reaches into her robes and pulls out a small bundled cloth. 'Archon, I found the concealment charm underneath your cot.'

He looks at it, takes it gently, and unwinds it to reveal something small and shiny. It's a silver watch with a digital inset. The hands are luminescent and glow in the dim light of the room. 'I'm sorry, Sarinne. I had to keep it. It's all I've got left of him since they took his journals and papers. I'm sorry.'

She looks at him sadly. 'No, you're not. You're too headstrong to truly know what you're playing with. We were ordered to surrender all his belongings, Archon, all of them. If the Guardians discover that you've kept anything back, you'll be sent to the Court.'

'They'll never know,' he says. 'I worked a concealment on the cloth, one I found in an ancient book. The Guardians don't know about it and they won't know to look for it.'

She reaches out and touches his cheek gently with a hand.

'I don't want to lose you, too,' she says. 'The Guardians will discover this sooner or later, as I did. You must turn it in or you'll risk being sent to trial. And I'll lose you, Archon, just as I lost him.'

He bows his head. 'Tomorrow, I promise.'

I see myself, lying in the bed, looking pale and thin and very much unlike myself. My hair has faded to the colour of dead leaves. I look like a statue. Like an ice sculpture. I look like one of *them*, the people of Shar.

Archon gasps, pulls back. 'I'm . . . I'm sorry,' he stutters, horrified.

'What is that?' I ask urgently.

'What? Keira, what happened?' Daniel calls. 'Are you okay?'

'Yes. No,' I answer, confused. 'I saw you, Archon. You were in a room full of books. Your mother was there. I heard you . . . what was that?'

'You felt the *ihlwarh?*' He seems amazed. 'But you're human. You're not supposed to be able to do that. It's impossible!'

'Well, obviously, it's not!'

'But in everything I've read, it's said that humans are incapable of using the *ihlwarh*. It requires years of practice to control it properly . . .'

'Control *what?* What did I just do?'

Still stunned, he rubs his hands, as if trying to instil some feeling in them. 'The *ihlwarh* is a . . . joining of minds. It's a very private thing. We are all schooled carefully in keeping it controlled.'

'Then what just happened?' I ask.

'I don't know.' He looks even more excited now than he did before. 'But this is incredible! If this works, you could share more with me about your world. I could experience your experiences, see what you've seen.' His eyes gleam. 'Keira, give me your hand –'

'No.' I pull my hand back, curling it to my chest. Who knows what touching him again will do to me? I have to get out of here. I have to get home before I change completely. I want my room and my bed and Molly and Mum. I don't want to be here, I don't want to be one of them, I want –

I freeze suddenly as I realise something.

'Archon,' I say. 'I need to find the thing I lost in your garden. The telescope.'

He stops, looking at me as if I've just given him a present and decided to take it back. I refuse to let it bug me. *I'm not his lab experiment*, I remind myself. *I don't owe him anything.*

'Your device,' he says, still sounding wounded. 'I told you, I don't know what happened to it.'

'It's the only chance we've got of getting back,' I tell him. 'We need to find it.'

I'm grateful when he takes a step back, although I still feel like a mean kid dangling some precious thing just out of reach.

'We have monitoring devices in the Etherium but nothing like what you've described. I've heard of such things, but only the Guardians have access to them. I don't know how you could have come across it in your world.'

That knot of guilt in my stomach clenches tighter. I don't want to tell him how I had "come across" it.

'It's special,' Daniel says from his bed. 'It's the only one on Earth.' Am I wrong, or is there an accusing edge to his voice?

Choosing to ignore his tone, I fix my gaze on Archon, trying to let him know how important it is. 'I need to find it.'

'You want to go home,' he says, and his voice is sympathetic. 'I know. Keira, Daniel, I promise you both, I'll do my best. But in the meantime, you will help me, won't you? I'll let you rest for a bit. I'm expected at the Etherium, but I'll return soon, and we can continue our discussion.'

After a pause, he adds, 'Keira? I'm very glad you came here.'

I turn away and lie down. He doesn't care that I might never see my world again. Why should he? He's not the one who's stranded halfway across the galaxy in a universe he's never dreamed of.

Chapter 13
The Guardians

AFTER a long while, I look across at Daniel. Just like me, he's awake and looking at the ceiling.

I can feel the restraint pressing down on me. My fingers ache. I make the slightest of movements and savour the relief as the heaviness falls away. I'm free.

I slip my legs over the side of the bed. Archon has conveniently left my crutches leaning against the wall within arm's reach. I grab them.

'What are you doing?' Daniel whispers.

'I've got to look for the telescope,' I say. 'And the bridge. We have to get out of here, Daniel. You heard what Archon said. They think we're dangerous, and even if Archon and his mum don't mean us any harm, I don't like the sound of those Guardians.'

Not to mention Arina. That girl that makes me very nervous.

'But if they *do* mean us harm,' Daniel protests, 'maybe it's best not to make them angry? Shouldn't we just stay here?' I can hear the tremor in his voice. He's afraid of the Guardians, just like I am. But unlike him, my fear makes me angry.

'You can stay if you want,' I retort. But it's a bluff, one I'm pretty sure he won't call. If he's that scared of the Guardians, he'll follow me for sure. Besides, I can't leave him behind. What would Jake say if I abandoned his little brother?

I'm already working on Daniel's restraints, picking them apart with my fingers. It surprises me how easily I can do this now. I can feel the edges of the blanket almost as clearly as the material of my grey gown. All I have to do is lift it and pull and it comes away quickly. Daniel sits up, wide-eyed.

'How do you do that?' he asks, because he has to question everything.

I don't have time to answer. 'Come on,' I order him, hoisting myself onto my crutches. He follows obediently, just as I hoped he would, and I lead the way across the room to the door. We pause while I look left and right, but I already know there's no one there. My senses are tingling; it feels like little rivers of lemonade are running underneath my skin.

You're human, Archon had said. *It's supposed to be impossible.*

But it's not. Somehow, I'm becoming part of the city and it's becoming part of me. I'm turning into a Sharian.

'This way,' I say confidently, manoeuvring myself and my crutches to the left. Daniel tags along behind, uncertainly. 'Hey,' I tell him. 'Remember the game we used to play? Explorers on the Moon?'

His cheeks go a bit red. I guess he's probably at the stage where he doesn't like being reminded that, not too long ago, he liked playing make-believe games.

'This is totally like that, but so much cooler, right?'

Daniel gives a faint grin.

'Why didn't you and Jake tell me about this?' I ask. I don't mean to sound accusing, but I do. 'About Shar and the telescope.'

'It wasn't just you. We didn't tell anyone. And anyway, would you have believed us?'

We reach the end of the hallway, and I see light spilling from the windows in front of us. I head for them, assuming there might be a way out.

'No, probably not.' I answer him. 'At least, not until I saw the telescope. But you could have said something after that.'

'I would have. But it was important to keep it a secret,' Daniel says.

'Why was it so important?' Frustrated, I stop moving to look at him and deliver the glare I usually save for the opposing soccer team before a game, hoping to scare him into an explanation. But he doesn't back down.

'It's just . . . because,' he says, 'it's something very important. I don't want to say anything about it now.' He looks around warily, and I think I understand. He's scared someone will overhear us. And he's not just scared for himself which means that there's something, or some*one*, else he's protecting.

I smile, because I admire him for that. He's got guts.

The windows open out into an open walkway, which leads into a small courtyard. *Is this the same garden I fell into when the bridge collapsed?* It looks the same. There are those star-shaped white flowers, planted in neatly-edged garden beds, and a few tall white trees with tiny white leaves. A small fountain trickles misty *vinarhi* over a series of steps. The pavement is immaculate, except for one area, near the bubbling fountain, where a black scorch-mark mars the surface of the stone.

Bingo.

I move over to the spot, and Daniel comes up beside me. For a moment we just stand there, looking down at the black mark, as if we can make the bridge reappear by sheer will alone.

'You can do magic, like the Sharians,' Daniel says. 'Can you make it come back?'

I've been wondering that myself. I balance on my crutches and try to feel with my hands. There *is* something there and it snags on my fingers like a sheet of cling-wrap. I twist my hand, trying to push through it, and something pinches my fingertips.

'Hey, something's happening!' Daniel says. He points at the air in front of us. It's starting to look hazy. *I'm doing it,* I realise. *I'm making a bridge!*

The air clears a little. For a moment I can see something moving in the trickling *vinarhi*. It's a reflection of the sky overhead. It's . . . they're *lights*! Hundreds and thousands of them, twinkling, and yellow and warm. The lights of our world.

Then, the boundary snaps back and the force of a speeding car hits me right in the chest. I'm hurled backwards and I skid to a stop near the walkway, my ankle exploding with pain. I'm vaguely aware of Daniel rushing to my side and yelling for help but everything is fading fast.

I almost had it. What happened? I think, before falling into blackness.

***

I drift in a half-sleep. I'm dreaming Molly is licking my hand when I hear the voices.

' . . . contacted you. I apologise —'

'Save your words! This will . . .'

'Please. You can check my record over the past years.' This voice is definitely Sarinne's, and I can hear their footsteps now. The silhouettes of several people appear outside my room. 'You won't find any new infractions. I have been pronounced "reformed".'

'That will count for nothing given the magnitude of this infringement. The fact that your own daughter has performed the honourable task of reporting this matter only strengthens the case against you.'

I blink groggily. I'm back in the sick room, lying on the bed. Daniel is in his bed, too, looking nervously towards the partition. The footsteps come closer and a tall woman rounds the corner into the room. I hate her instantly. She has a long, beak-like nose and hard, cold eyes. She wears a pale green robe and a blue sash. Three others follow her, two men and another woman.

From my dreams, I instinctively know that these people are the all-powerful Guardians. Their robes signify their various Guilds and their sashes indicate their rank. Colours have so much meaning here.

Blue for Healers, I remember. *Red for Arbitrators of Justice. Yellow for Overseers. Purple, like Archon's sash, for Etherologists or scientists.*

All four of them are tall, cold, and pale.

Behind them comes Sarinne, she looks furious, but more than a bit scared.

'They are both young,' says the Healer.

'Their age makes no difference. Even a young human can be extremely dangerous,' says the beak-nosed woman.

'I agree. But there is something about the girl that is especially unusual . . .'

The Healer closes his eyes and raises his hands in the air. His fingers move as if taking pieces of invisible thread, winding it around and through something. Watching him, I remember doing the same thing years ago when I was making the base of our treehouse, using rope to tie the separate bits of wood together to make something solid.

'The reports from the Etherium suggested an incursion, but the disturbance was so brief they couldn't detect the location of the bridge. But just look at her, Guardian Rashae! The boy looks human but she certainly doesn't. And her aura . . .' He trails off, shaking his head.

'The sooner we get them to the Chambers, the sooner we can explore the reasons. As for you . . .' Guardian Rashae turns on Sarinne, her hard eyes glaring more coldly than before, 'you will be called upon to answer for your transgressions. You and your son both.'

I can't hold my tongue any longer. 'Hey! Don't blame him for not telling you we arrived,' I say. 'I threatened him! I said I'd shoot them with my demon powers. Sarinne, Archon, Arina . . . all of them!'

All five snap their gazes on me. I stare back as confidently as I can.

'It's true!' Daniel shouts from across the room. 'We've got tanks and everything on Earth that I can call up whenever we want. And we'll shoot you too, if you try to punish them! They were only helping us!'

'Child,' says Sarinne, her voice softer than before, 'quiet. This isn't necessary.'

'Just try us, then,' I say, glaring at the

Guardians. 'Go on! I mean, Sarinne had us both under a restraining aura, right? They were trying to keep us here until they could get help.'

But nothing I say seems to make a difference. I might as well be shouting at a brick wall.

'Illortha,' says Guardian Rashae, completely ignoring me, 'Work a motion charm. We must get this one to the Chambers as soon as possible.'

The Healer, Illortha, shakes his head imperceptibly. 'The strangeness of her aura is disturbing.'

'She is *human*.' Guardian Rashae utters the word as if it's a synonym for *poop*.

'It's more than that ... ' Illortha says. He gestures towards me and Guardian Rashae frowns, carefully examining face.

'She does have the appearance of –'

'One of us,' says Sarinne in a low voice. 'See the traces of ice on her skin? The silver tinge to her hair? It's been growing more pronounced! I've examined human travellers before. The auras I've studied are distinct. Even if they spend time in Shar, they remain obvious. This one is different. Her colour is not clear; she seems to move between yellow, red and purple, mixing all of them and blurring at the edges.'

'Hello! I'm right here!' I say. Yeah, it's probably not a great idea to antagonise these people, but I figure that if I keep their attention on me, it'll distract them from Archon and Daniel.

Maybe I can keep them safe.

But again, my words fall on deaf ears. Guardian Rashae turns her back on me to speak to Illortha. 'Can you work the charm?'

Apparently, Illortha can. He raises his hands and weaves them through the air, flicking his fingers in precise movements. I watch him, thinking of the invisible threads I'd felt when I moved the restraints, or tried to make the bridge. He looks like one of those street mimes they're supposed to have in France; but whatever he's doing isn't pretend because I feel the heaviness lift from my body.

'You can stand,' instructs Rashae. 'You will be able to walk, but be warned; you have a compulsion placed upon you. We use the same process when transporting criminals. If you try to escape, you'll be immobilised and it will cause you great pain.'

'Oh, so I'm a criminal?'

Rashae levels her cold stare at me. 'Stand. Don't try to walk yet. Illortha will need to make some adjustments.'

I push myself up. Amazingly, everything seems to work. Still cautious, I slip over the edge of the bed, half expecting to fall again, but amazingly I'm standing without any pain in my ankle. How awesome is this?

Imagine if we had this kind of treatment on Earth. What else can they do? Cure cancer? HIV?

Guardian Illortha has his eyes closed and

he's making more movements. 'Please try and take a step,' he says after a moment.

I do. And it works. I can move. I can freaking *walk*.

I almost burst into tears. It's a wonderful feeling.

I'm free.

Free.

Before I think about it, I launch myself towards Daniel and, this time, I don't *lift* the restraining blanket but tear it away from him, feeling it shred under my fingers.

'Run!' I yell at Daniel. He doesn't need to be told twice and jumps off the bed. He races towards the door, dodging the Guardians with the kind of seasoned skills of a professional soccer midfielder.

The Guardians are taken by surprise but, strangely, none of them reach out to physically stop him or block his path. The Sharians don't seem to be keen on touching each other, let alone a rogue human, and I'm only one step behind Daniel. It feels great to run, but my heart is pounding with fear as well. At any moment the Guardians will probably blast us with thunderbolts or something. Besides which, I'm not even sure which way to go.

Daniel darts left into a familiar corridor, it's the same one we came down before, leading out to the courtyard.

'No! We'll be trapped!' I yell at him. Is he hoping the bridge will have miraculously reappeared? There's no way I'm going to try plunging through that barrier again. Being hurled across the garden once was enough.

'The water!' Daniel gasps over his shoulder. I have no idea what he's talking about until we break out into the courtyard and he runs across to the trickling stone fountain. Then I see what he's up to. The water, the *vinarhi*, runs across the flat steps and down through an arched gap in the courtyard wall. Why didn't I see that before?

Daniel drops onto the lowest step in the fountain and scrambles through the hole on his hands and knees. I chance a look behind me and see several figures close on my heels. Rashae, her face twisted in anger, Illortha, looking strained from the hurried sprint and Sarinne, wide-eyed with hope and panic. That's all I need to spur me on. I dive after Daniel.

My ankle doesn't hurt but I don't know if that's a good sign or a bad one. Like Arina said, there's no telling what damage might be caused by putting pressure on it like this. But I can't stop. The *vinarhi* washes over me with the same bubbling, fresh feeling as it did in the bathroom. It's shallow, and I can feel the smooth, cool stone underneath. The smell of violets is overwhelming in the enclosed space. I crawl forwards. I'm bigger than Daniel and my robe snags on the edges of the gap in the wall but then I'm through and out in the world of Shar.

Chapter 14
Fugitives

'LOOK!' Daniel gasps, pointing. I'm not sure what he's pointing at exactly. Maybe everything. There's so much to see.

It's been so long since I've been outside that I feel overwhelmed when I see the sky.

But the sky is so different. There's an openness to it. It's a darker colour than it should be, almost purple. The stars are the same stars I would see at home, but I've never seen them so clear and close before.

And beyond them . . .

I can see it. My world. Just like the satellite images of Earth from above. I can make out Indonesia, New Zealand, and Australia, all picked out in glowing gold lights.

It's still there. I feel tears prickle my eyes. I want to reach out and touch it, but all I can do is look.

I shiver. The air is chilly and I remember this is how it's supposed to be here.

From outside, Sarinne's house looks like a fairytale cottage squashed inwards and stretched upwards, except that it's mostly white and faintly mottled with blue. On either side are similar buildings with balconies, wide open windows, terraced gardens and turreted roofs.

I listen to the sounds of people walking, the distant murmur of voices. There is no whoosh of traffic, no police sirens, no chatter from nearby TVs. Daniel is gazing around stunned. There isn't a single advertising poster or neon light in sight. There are no trains, no bikes. No technology at all.

'Come on,' I say, wrenching both of us back to the present, and the very real danger we're facing. The Guardians will be coming after us at any moment. We have to get out of here.

I grab Daniel's hand. He feels warm and solid, comfortingly human under my cold fingers. I don't want to lose him out here, how would we ever find each other again? I pull him to the right, down a long street lined with houses. There are a few Sharians walking in the opposite direction, all wearing long robes with sashes of different colours, and our appearance makes them pause and stare. Their gaze slides over me, because even though my sash is plain, in my long grey robe I look Sharian. They look at Daniel, who is clearly *not* one of them. We're both shaking the fizzing drips of *vinarhi* from our long robes, and little wisps flow from our fingertips and bare feet but, despite our dishevelled appearance, none of the onlookers approach us. I can't tell if they're stunned or afraid. Maybe both.

Daniel looks left and right. 'We need to get to the Etherium,' he says, pointing. 'I think it was that way, but it's hard to tell. It all looks different from down here!'

That's true. From the windows of the house, when Archon pointed out the Etherium, we were looking down at the city. From ground level, everything is rising up above us, obscuring the view. But that doesn't matter to me. In my mind is a printed map of the city, and I know the way. But how . . .

'Why the Etherium?' I ask, 'There will be more Guardians there!'

'Yes, but didn't you hear Archon? That's where they monitor the Ether. That's where they can detect changes. That's where –'

He doesn't need to finish the sentence. 'We can find another bridge!' And, I add silently, we can find Archon. 'You're brilliant, Daniel. Come on. This way.'

I don't turn to look over my shoulder, that would take too much time and I'm afraid of what I might see. Instead we dash across the glassy pavement, leaving fading footprints of *vinarhi* behind us along with the bewildered onlookers.

'How can you know which way to go?' Daniel pants behind me.

Saying *I just remember, that's all*, doesn't seem quite satisfactory, even to me; so I just run and hope he trusts me enough to follow.

The streets are long and wide, but there are stairs and back alleys that lead between the buildings. I try to take as many turns as possible, to put our pursuers far behind us, but I know in my heart that they will be able to trace us, no matter how fast we run. They have the advantage of their magic. *Our* only advantage is speed, but that's not something I've ever had a problem with, at least, not before I broke my ankle. Now, with the magic spell supporting me, I pound up a winding pathway and across a narrow walkway, passing doors and windows and just a few startled Sharian faces, Daniel on my heels.

We come out into an open space. It's paved at the edges, but in the centre is a square of pale green grass. A couple of seats are set beneath half-a-dozen of those strange white trees. There are people here, sitting and talking in low voices, or holding open books on their laps.

I stop, not wanting to plunge into the middle of them, and Daniel crashes into me from behind. We can't go barrelling out into the open, or we'll attract their attention. I'm about to look for another way around when I see a group of four standing in the centre of the park, two adults and two younger girls who are dressed in Novice robes like Arina's.

One of the older women is speaking. ' . . . ensure that the place selected has been properly prepared. This can be confirmed by any

Overseer's reports. No building will take place unless it has been approved by the proper authorities.'

'Beira, you may plant the seed crystal,' says the other woman.

One of the girls steps forward, holding something in her hand. As she crouches, she closes her eyes and places what she is holding carefully on the ground. Instantly, something blossoms out of it, like one of those time-lapse videos in nature documentaries showing a plant growing over a series of months, in all a few seconds.

Long white tentacles fold out and spread across the crisp grass. The older women circle. 'Keep your focus. Remember to contain every part of it. It will take its own shape, but you must be a guide for it.'

Little stems, like plant stalks, unfurl and twist upwards, making thin pillars. As they reach towards the sky they expand outwards as well, thickening into solid supports. Curling threads spread out between them, patterned like iron-lace. Finally, a roof appears, capping the whole thing.

'Wow,' I whisper. It's a rotunda. They grew a rotunda.

'Excellent work,' one of the Overseers says.

'I wish I could do that,' Daniel whispers.

I nod. I do too. But we don't have time to stand around and gawk.

I point to the left. We head down an alley-way and turn right at the next corner where a tall, turreted building looms above us, looking like a medieval castle carved out of ice.

'Is that it?' Daniel says in an awed gasp.

I nod. 'The Etherium,' I say, and give him a little push in the direction of the nearest door. It's an archway and it's open. I wonder for a moment if they have any locks in Shar, but when I try to step through the archway I realise that they have a different way of protecting their property. A shiver passes through me. I feel like someone's peeled my skin back and had a look at my innards. The feeling is gone just as quickly and I know I've passed some kind of test.

Daniel isn't so lucky.

He puts one foot on the doorstep and an invisible force knocks him backwards. 'Ah!' he shouts.

'What? What is it?' I ask worriedly. 'Are you alright?'

'Something hit me,' he replies, sitting up. He puts his hand into the doorway and pulls it back just as quickly. 'I don't think I can enter.'

I raise my hands and try to feel for the force. If it's anything like the restraints on the beds, I can just lift it away. But there's a sudden sound from behind me. Voices. Someone's coming!

'There's no time,' Daniel hisses. 'You go in.'

'I can't leave you –'

'Don't worry, I'll hide.' Daniel turns back towards the park. 'Just find Archon, and be quick!'

I look over my shoulder and see shadows of approaching people. It's too late to do anything except run.

'Be careful!' I whisper, and walk quickly in the opposite direction. The corridor is long and the crystal-like walls are patterned with floral swirls. Up ahead, more people cross through an adjoining hallway. I lower my head so that my almost-silver hair covers my face.

I remember what Archon told me, when he showed us the Etherium. *That's where I work, on the second floor . . .*

I need to go up. There are steps at the end of this hallway, hanging in a suspended spiral. I put my foot on the first step warily, but it feels solid, and I begin to climb.

I emerge into a wide hall.

It's incredible.

The ceiling is domed and, at the highest point of the dome are five or six little openings set in a circle. *Vinarhi* pours through these inlets, each stream joining together in a cascade of silver light, and the smell of violets fills the air. The *vinarhi* falls into a recessed pool in the centre of the room where it runs through small channels carved like snail trails into the floor. Little tendrils of misty light reach up from these, coiling around the feet of Sharians who are gathered in groups at the edges of the hall. Others are bent over the roadmap of light, trailing their fingers through the *vinarhi* and cupping handfuls every now and then, only to let it trickle back. They do all this with looks of careful concentration.

One man looks up towards me. My heart skips a beat.

What are you so scared of, Keira? I ask myself. *You've never been this worried about doing something daring before.* But I know what it is. It's not just me I'm putting in danger by doing this. Daniel is out there, relying on me.

I drop my head, letting my pale hair fall over my face, and tentatively take a step forwards. No one looks up, so I take another. And another. It reminds me of crossing the ice bridge, but this is far scarier. There's nothing calling me now, just the opposite, in fact. Every instinct is screaming at me to run the other way.

But I manage to reach the centre of the hall and I realise no one is looking at me. No one is shouting out in alarm, or pointing at me, and I realise something else. If I wasn't supposed to be here, the guarding spells on the doors would have kept me out, like they did Daniel. So everyone assumes I'm a Sharian, and that I'm allowed in.

I tell myself to stop worrying. The boost of confidence is all I need, and I walk the rest of the way easily. I start to feel a bit more like my old cocky self and I welcome the familiar feeling, which is refreshing. Before I can think too much about it, I march right up to the nearest Sharian, he's wearing a long robe with a purple sash, so I know he's an Etherologist.

He's cupping a handful of *vinarhi*, and I can see it swirling and resettling in his palm.

He looks up as I approach, and the *vinarhi* runs through his fingers. He raises his hand and turns it towards me. Instinctively, I put my hand out, and the *vinarhi* pours into my own palm.

It feels cool and tickles slightly. Then it starts to move, slowly, as if it's being stirred with a spoon.

'The unsettling has got much worse,' he murmurs. It's as if he's talking to himself. 'I've never seen anything like it.'

'What, um, what is causing it?' I ask him, but he shakes his head.

'I've never seen such disturbances. There are records of such things, but nothing in my lifetime. I'm due to make a report but I don't know what to say.'

'I'm looking for Archon,' I interrupt. Will he notice that I'm only wearing a plain sash? But I'm a pretty good actor sometimes, even if I do say so myself. My voice comes out soft but commanding, just like a Sharian's.

'The First Level record-keeper?' he replies, and, when I nod curtly, he turns towards the far door. 'Down the first corridor, make a right turn. The last door will lead you to the record-keeper's office.'

I don't thank him, because I have a feeling these people aren't big on thanking each other. I let the rest of the *vinarhi* trickle through my fingers and splash back into the channels on the floor. The man is already turning away to gather more.

I make it to the doorway, the smell of violets in my nostrils, and enter another long corridor. I follow it to the end, taking a moment to touch the walls where beautiful patterns of trees, vines, and leaves swirl just below its cold, glassy surface. The last door is small and covered with one of those shimmering curtains tucked into the corner, as if it wasn't important enough to make it noticeable.

I step through the curtain and find myself in a larger space than I expected. The room extends upwards through three levels of balconied galleries, each wall lined with shelves that are shaped differently to accommodate their contents. There are scrolls, rolled neatly and stacked atop one another. There are sheafs of thin, pure white paper, tucked in rectangular divisions. And books, thousands of books, line the rest of the room in all shapes and sizes. They're bound with cloth and covered with jackets of thick paper. The titles are written in an alphabet I don't recognise, and yet I can read them. *A Treatise on Matter, Study of Minor Disturbances, Discourse in Parallel Theory* . . .

I can hear someone moving behind one of the shelves. I keep close to the wall and circle around, hearing voices as I draw closer.

' . . . have searched everywhere, but the best texts have been moved.' It's Archon. 'I could only find information dating from many, many years ago, and it doesn't tell us what we need to know. It would help if we were given access to the confiscated material . . .'

Another deeper voice intercedes. 'Those texts are off-limits, Ensign.'

'I know that, but I'm sure if we were given access –'

The voice cuts him off. 'Are you questioning the judgement of the Guardians?'

'No, of course not!' Archon sounds flustered. 'But . . . we already know these kinds of fluctuations have been recorded before, that's clear from the bits and pieces we've managed to gather from the books and scrolls here, and if we can only find out where, when and how they compare to what the monitors are finding now, we might be able to give them the answers they want!'

The response is terse. 'I do not want you wasting time with these questions. Just do as you've been asked.'

As footsteps recede into the distance I press myself close to the wall and peer around the edge of a shelf. I see Archon standing in front of a wide desk that is covered with sheets of paper and open books. His back is to me and he is clenching his fists.

'Psst!' I hiss.

He whirls, knocking some of the papers to the floor. When he sees me, his eyes go wide. 'Keira?'

He looks quickly over his shoulder in the direction his colleague must have gone, then dashes across to me. His hands are raised and for a second I think he means to hug me. It's only at the last moment he stops, remembering what happened the last time we touched.

'What are you doing here?' he whispers. 'How did you get out of bed?'

'They, your Guardians, worked some kind of magic spell on me.'

'Magic!' he smiles at my use of the word. 'It's not magic. It was a motion charm. And a good one if you managed to walk all this way. But how did you find me? Why have you come here?' Suddenly the smile fades. 'What's wrong? Why did the Guardians come to the house?'

'They know about us. Me and Daniel. I remember you said they would know we arrived, but how could they have figured out where we were so soon?'

A dark look crosses Archon's face. 'Arina. She probably told them.' His knuckles turn white as he clenched his fists again. 'I should have known! She's too ambitious for her own good! She doesn't realise what they'll do to Mother and I. Or . . . or to you.'

I shiver. 'We have to get out of here, Archon. They want to take us to the Chambers, and even though they're talking about healing my leg, I'm pretty sure I don't want to go there.'

'No, you don't,' he agrees sombrely. 'They will heal you, but once you're inside, they won't let you leave. Something big is happening, and they know it. I think you're a part of it. We have to find a way –'

'Ensign Archon. Step away from the human.'

The voice is loud, authoritative. Archon obediently steps back. I turn slowly, dreading what I'm going to see and there they are, Guardian Rashae at the head, striding into the room. They surround us quickly and efficiently.

I move to put myself in front of Archon. He looks so unusual amidst these tall, calm figures. I hadn't realised before exactly how much his physical appearance sets him apart, but it's clear now . . . now that they've mentioned how much I look like one of them. He looks . . . he looks almost *human.*

He speaks frantically from behind me. 'The girl is wounded. Her leg is badly injured. It's festering with some kind of infection and further damaged by her escape attempt. We were treating her . . .'

But Guardian Rashae answers him calmly. 'She will receive the *proper* treatment in the Healer's Hall. Ensign Archon, are you aware that you are already facing charges of disobeying the Edict?'

He hangs his head. 'Yes, Guardian Rashae.'

'You should have bought this to our attention immediately. We are well aware of your record, Ensign. This is another transgression. Your superiors will be informed. You will be facing serious consequences.'

Archon does a pretty good impression of a deflating balloon. He seems to hunch in on himself. Anger flushes through me, but it's not the red-hot temper that I usually feel. This time there's an edge to it, like a cold knife.

'Leave him alone. It's me you want. He's got nothing to do with this.'

But somehow, I know nothing that will convince them of that.

'Search the building,' Rashae commands the other Guardians. 'Every inch of it. When you find the boy, inform me immediately.'

Chapter 15
The Chambers

EVERYTHING becomes a blur as I'm led out of the room. The Guardians march me down the corridor, taking a left turn instead of a right to avoid the large hall I came in through, down a flight of stone stairs and through an arched doorway into the open street.

I can see people walking on the bridges above us. Ahead, a railing edges the pathway on which we stand and, if I was to look over the edge, I know I'd see the levels below filled with more of the same orderly pedestrians. I don't get a chance, though. The Guardians are in a hurry.

They still won't touch me. Is this something to do with the *lhlwarh*? Maybe they don't want to taint their minds through contact with mine. Instead they walk on either side of me, my own personal escorts. But even if they don't want to touch me, they're not about to let me run off again.

I try to look around without attracting their attention. Inside, I'm frantic. *Where is Daniel?*

Does he know I've been caught? Rashae says nothing. I can only hope Daniel has enough sense to stay hidden and won't go looking for me when I don't show up. At least one of us will be safe.

I can see other Guardians around us, stopping people in the streets to question them. As we pass the garden park, with its newly added rotunda, two Guardians approach the group of Novices.

'There is a human boy hiding nearby,' one of them states in a clear voice. 'Have you seen him?'

The Novices freeze in place. Their eyes are downcast, but I can see them glancing sideways at one another when the Guardians aren't looking.

'No, Guardian Geardil,' says one of the Guardians who had instructed the girl on how to use the seed crystal earlier. 'But if we notice anything unusual, we will report it immediately.'

'I saw . . .' one of the girls says and my heart jumps, 'something in the shadows, just at the edge of the park. As if hiding from view. I thought I was imagining things and I didn't want to be distracted . . .'

Rashae does not allow me to linger and hear the rest. 'Come!' she barks at me, and I'm led onwards.

Just past the garden is a paved platform with steps leading up to a long walkway suspended by arched pillars. Below us is a dizzying drop, a chasm between buildings. At the bottom is a haze of the *vinarhi*, the river; a brilliant white that swirls and eddies like mist.

I stop to look over the railing. The Guardians walking on either side of me are forced to stop too. 'What's down there?' I ask Rashae in a loud voice.

She turns to me, annoyed at the interruption.

'I mean,' I continue, hoping that my questions will distract her from thinking about Daniel and myself from worrying, 'where does the water go? It must flow somewhere. You don't have any oceans. Where does it end up?'

'That is not your concern.' She frowns and, with a flash of double-vision, I can see her aura, and the flickering of an annoyed yellow-green within it tells me that she doesn't know the answer.

In a softer voice, she adds, 'Humans have developed a curious way of thinking. There is no direction when it comes to realities. Space is not a linear thing, and what it contains can exist in more than one place at a time. The *vinarhi* runs between the worlds. Just as bridges create links between them, the *vinarhi* keeps them separate. I cannot tell you any more than that. There are some secrets that have been lost over time. That is one of them.'

It kind of makes sense, but again, only if I don't think about it too much. The *vinarhi* is down there, but Earth is above us. The person I remember being in my dreams, the Sharian who knows about *vinarhi* and bridges and the Ether can accept this. It's only my human mind that struggles.

'But you work the Ether,' I say. 'If you can make it do stuff for you, like help people walk, then you should know what it's made of. If you examined it properly, wouldn't that tell you everything you need to know?'

'That's not possible,' she informs me. 'The foundations, the *hallichar*, are protected from our probing by their very nature. The boundaries are thin down there. The currents are so erratic it's impossible to read them.'

She starts to walk again, and I reluctantly pull away from the railing.

'Hey,' I say, as my escort falls in around me once more. 'You're not really going to punish Archon, are you?'

'Ensign Archon will be called to face the consequences of his actions.'

'But he didn't do anything wrong –' I argue, but she cuts me off with a cold glare.

'He has several serious infractions on his record already. The accident of his birth gives him some excuse. His emotions are unpredictable, his manners impulsive, but we can't ignore another infringement.'

'What do you mean? What are you talking about . . . his birth?' I have a feeling this has something to do with what Archon was hiding from me. I'm desperate to find out what it is. I remember Archon saying something about his heritage being a curse. Could this be it?

'Archon is partly human,' Rashae replies, taking obvious pleasure in revealing this little bit of information to me. 'His mother was . . . *involved* . . . with a traveller from your world several years ago, a man named Frederick Mason.'

'A man from my world?' My heart starts beating double-time. Another traveller from Earth, who came here . . . was he stranded, like I was? Where was he now? I try desperately to remember everything Archon had said about his father, but I don't remember much at all.

'He came across a bridge, like you did,' Rashae continues. 'But we managed to intercept him before he could cause any damage.'

'What kind of damage could he have caused? He was probably just a normal person, like me!' Frederick Mason, it's such a normal name. In my mind, I can see an older version of Archon, with the same sandy hair and kind eyes. The man I see in my head, I can't picture him being a danger to anyone.

'He was imprisoned in the cells,' Rashae continues, 'for his own safety and the safety of Shar.'

'And Sarinne met him there while she was working with the prisoners,' I conclude.

Rashae nods. 'Sarinne has redeemed herself since, but the son that resulted from their relationship seems to have inherited far too many *human* tendencies. A few years ago it was discovered that he was hiding certain artefacts; objects that had belonged to his father, dangerous technology from your world. He was only saved from trial because he turned them in himself. But we can't overlook his actions now. His infringements are endangering the city.'

'He's not endangering the city by learning about my world,' I argue. 'That's just your opinion because you want to keep all the power for yourselves.'

I wish I hadn't said that. My stupid mouth seems to have a mind of its own sometimes.

'You know nothing about our world or our laws!' Rashae silences me with a voice like ice and marches on ahead. It's clear she doesn't intend to continue the discussion.

It takes fifteen minutes to cross the walkway. I've been so busy looking around that I haven't noticed where we're going. When my feet hit the bottom step of a spiralling staircase, I realise we've actually been heading towards one of the surrounding outer towers of the huge complex Archon told me about. The Chambers.

We climb, and the towering buildings loom over us. The shadows cast by them are thick and deep, the strange crystal walls giving off only a dull glow down here. We cross a paved area towards a doorway set into the base of the nearest tower. It's made out of panes of clear crystal and swings open as we approach to reveal a wide atrium. The floor is tiled with smooth cream-coloured stone. A sweeping stairway leads upwards and tall windows on either side let in the brilliant white light. A desk, made out of the familiar metal-wood material, runs along one wall. Behind it is a large open passageway that leads into blackness. A man emerges from it, looking grim, and comes up to the desk when he sees us enter.

My entourage disassembles itself. The second woman heads towards the desk, and speaks quickly to the man there. Illortha strides through one of the many doors that lead off to the sides. Rashae and the second man stay on either side of me until the other woman returns. Without another word, I'm led towards the stairs.

Even climbing these is easy. My ankle doesn't so much as twinge.

'So,' I ask, 'is this walking thing permanent? Can I keep the magic charm? Take it home with me?'

'Hardly,' says Rashae, making a sound somewhere between a huff and a snort. 'The charm has disguised the pain, but your wounds are significant. If you were to continue using your leg in this manner you'd only make the injury worse.'

'You could have just said "no",' I grumble. Geez, these Sharians really aren't big on optimism. 'Why wouldn't it work?'

'Your world is very different from Shar,' she explains, 'and there are forces there that counteract the strength of charms, and keep them from forming properly.'

'Counteracting forces? Like what?'

'Everything in this universe has a polar opposite. In the case of what you call magic, it is–'

'Science?' Score one for me, I've taken her by surprise. I can tell by the way her frown deepens. 'I was wondering why there aren't any cars here, or trains, or computers. I mean, it makes sense. You use magic instead.'

She purses her lips. 'We have no need for machines and technological devices; such things are forbidden.'

'But what would happen if someone had one?' I ask slyly. Of course, I'm thinking about my phone, and the fact that Arina has it in her possession. I'm also thinking that Rashae might be wrong and the two forces don't cancel each other out. Arina said she'd heard a voice coming through my phone. If that was true, then technology can work in Shar and their magic might just work on Earth.

'They would be brought before the Court to face trial, of course. The minimum sentence would be a loss of their position and demotion within their guild. It would be a serious offence. It would be noted on their record. They might even be sentenced to imprisonment –' She breaks off, pointing.

'Here,' she says, and I see we've arrived at a

high archway leading into a room with a conical ceiling. Like the rest of the building, it's beautiful, stately and grand, but it feels sterile. As we enter I see why.

It's a hospital ward, or something like an infirmary. Beds, just like the shelf in the room in Sarinne's house, are set in shallow alcoves around the room, separated by filmy curtains. One of them is occupied by a tall figure, covered to his shoulders by a thin sheet. I can see three other figures in the alcoves, dressed in long robes like Rashae and her companions, their blue sashes indicating they are Healers.

I think of Doctor Dracula. She'd probably feel very much at home here.

I'm directed into one of the beds. Reluctantly I do as they say, mainly because now that I've stopped moving, I feel insanely tired. Rashae is talking to the Healers, who peer at me intently, but I tune them out, looking instead at the tall figure in the bed next to mine. I'm shocked to realise that he's *old*.

Somehow, up till now, it had seemed like these people wouldn't pass middle age. Until this moment, I haven't seen anyone who looks older than forty. But this man is proof that the people of Shar aren't immortal.

I don't think I've ever been this close to a really old person before. My Grandma died when I was three, so I don't remember her. I watched Jake's mum get sick and I saw her the day before she died, when she was so pale and thin that she hardly looked like a person at all, but that was different. She was struggling and fighting to live. This old man is peaceful, resting. His aura is pale green which tells me he's just waiting for the inevitable.

As if my gaze woke him, he turns around, blinking his deep blue eyes at me.

'Ah,' he sighs. 'Welcome.'

'Thanks,' I say warily. It seems like a weird thing to say, and I can't help thinking there's a deeper meaning to his words. 'Welcome to where, exactly?'

His sharp cackle sounds like it should crack him wide open. 'To this place. The Chambers, the Sanatorium. Our world, I suppose. Welcome to Shar.'

I look down at myself, or what I can see under the thin sheet. 'You know I'm not from here?' I ask. I know I should be relieved that someone can still tell the difference between me and a true Sharian, but I feel a bit disappointed that the messy, tomboy part of me is still visible.

'My eyes still work, though the rest of me is slowly failing,' he replies, then makes a gruff sound in his throat that might be a laugh. 'And besides that, I heard the Healers talking about you before you arrived.'

'Great, so now I'm the subject of this week's gossip column.' I roll my eyes, but I'm slightly scared by the amount of attention I'm receiving. 'Is everyone talking about me?'

He makes that sound again. 'The Guardians don't hold their tongues in front of me, no need to, I guess, since I cannot leave the Sanatorium, but even the Guardians can't stop people from talking.'

I try to raise myself up on my elbow, but it's useless. I settle for tilting my head to one side so I can see him properly. 'Do the Guardians do anything else except threaten people?'

He huffs and turns aside.

'Oh, come on,' I say. I'm pushing him and I know it, I just want one of these Sharians to see what I see. That the Guardians sound like dictators and that disagreeing with them might be a good thing. 'Everyone's scared of these people. Don't you ever get sick of them trying to control what you think?'

He is staring at the ceiling, deliberately avoiding my eyes.

'You have it wrong.' He says slowly. 'A Guardian's role is to maintain the balance. They only do what is necessary to keep our world safe.'

I shake my head, this is useless. The Guardians know no one will disobey them, because the other Sharians are all too afraid to speak out, even in private.

And I'm trapped here, at their mercy.

Chapter 16
The Sanatorium

I TEST out whether I can climb back out of the bed, only to hit a wall. Literally. They've put another restraining charm on me. I wonder if I can remove this one as well but, before I can try, the Healers arrive; a young woman, not much older than me, and a boy who would be about thirteen by Earth's standards. Their faces are serious, but it's still hard for me not to think of them as kids.

This reminds me about Daniel and a surge of anxiety grips me.

'When was the last time you had any food?' asks the girl. She's carrying a thin square tablet about the size of an exercise book and she uses her finger to make a few quick marks on it, leaving behind white squiggles of writing.

'Um . . .' I remember the liquid Archon fed me. Strangely, I haven't felt hungry since then. I also haven't needed to use a toilet. I suppose I'm lucky my period isn't due any time soon . . .

'A while ago. Yesterday.'

The girl turns to the boy. 'Yuli, you should send a communication to the kitchens to make sure she's only given nutrient cubes. I'm not sure how her human systems will react –'

Strangely enough, it's not the thought of eating whatever "nutrient cubes" are that bothers me most.

'Keira,' I interject.

The girl turns back to me, looking shocked that I spoke to her without being questioned. 'I beg your pardon?'

'My name is Keira. Not "her".'

She blinks. I can tell what I've said makes no impression on her. 'My apologies.' She makes another note.

'The Guardians want to do a full internal examination,' says the boy, Yuli, 'and the results are supposed to be added to the archives.'

'Internal examination?' I wince. 'You're not going to autopsy me alive, are you?'

They continue to talk as if I'm not there, ignoring me to the point that I start to wonder whether I actually exist or not. 'It's been scheduled for later this afternoon,' the girl says.

'We're not allowed to take part?' Yuli asks. I catch a trace of disappointment in his voice, and I can almost see him pouting like a normal thirteen-year-old when he's been told to go to bed before the movie ends.

The girl shakes her head. 'We're not supposed to have unnecessary contact.'

'But she's already *had* contact,' Yuli goes on. He's looking at me far too eagerly, like he wants to poke me with a stick and see if I'll growl. 'They're saying the half-breed Etherologist used the *ihlwarh* on her . . .'

The girl sniffs. 'You shouldn't be listening to rumours.'

'How can I help it? Everyone in the Chambers is talking about him! I was there when they bought him in through the main gallery!' Yuli's eyes sparkle with barely suppressed excitement. 'I saw them both, him and the human boy, before they told us to move on. They said they were taking them to the prisons.'

My heart nearly stops. The human boy they're talking about can only be Daniel. They've found him and they've got both him and Archon here in the Chambers. My mind goes into overdrive. I need to find where the prisons are and work out a way of getting Daniel out. And what about Archon? Can I break him out somehow as well?

'The display was only meant as a warning, Yuli,' the girl scolds, 'they want to make an example of them both. The Guardians want people to know exactly what the half-breed did, and how dangerous it was.'

They're talking about Archon as if he's a criminal psychopath! Rashae had said he would face a trial, but I hadn't really thought about what that meant. To think of him actually being locked in the jail he'd told me about, somewhere deep under these buildings, is frightening.

'Hey,' I say, and Yuli looks towards me warily. 'What's going to happen to him? The . . . the half-breed.' I hate that word. 'What are they going to do to him?'

They both stand there, looking at me for a long moment. Neither of them gives me an answer. I'm starting to feel more and more like a wild animal chained up in a zoo.

'What about her leg?' Yuli asks after a moment. 'Is it safe to examine her?'

'No. We're only supposed to evaluate her,' the girl replies. 'Another Novice has been assigned to the examination.'

The boy leans over me, moving his hands, just like Illortha had when he worked that magic walking charm on me.

'She's green-tinged red,' he says, 'mostly energy, movement, and impatience. But there's a . . . there's *more* colours swirling around her. It's almost like she's . . . not just one person. She's made up of parts of *everything*.'

He pauses, leaning closer, and I can see that he's half-amazed, half-terrified.

'It's as if she's not just one of them,' he add, almost in a whisper. 'Not just human. She's one of us as well.'

'Are you sure?' The girl pauses in making her notations to peer at me closely. Obviously this has shocked her. 'I mean . . . no. Humans are not supposed to ... their thoughts are closed. I don't understand.'

'Guardian Rashae didn't say anything about this.'

'She wouldn't, would she?' the girl says, looking a little worried. 'Don't say anything about reading her colours, Yuli. You weren't supposed to, and if they find out, they won't be happy.'

Yuli looks scared. It's probably the most real emotion I've seen on any Sharian's face, besides Archon's.

Archon. The half-breed. If he is half-human, then that's probably where that emotion comes from.

Archon. I realise I've come to think of him as a friend. How is that possible? I've only known him, what, two days? Have I been here that long? But it feels as if I've known him longer, somehow. It's more than the fact that he's probably my only ally in this world. I actually *miss* him. I wish he was here so I could talk to him. It doesn't matter if he's only interested in hearing about computers or picking my brains for information about my world. I like the way talking to him makes me feel. It's as if I'm really something special.

And now he's in serious trouble, and I can't do a thing to help him.

The two Novice Healers leave me after a few more minutes, but Yuli returns later with a tray of food. I'd been expecting army rations or something like that, but there's no sign of the nutrient cubes the girl Healer spoke about. Instead, there's a bowl of thick soup that somehow smells like both corn and strawberries at the same time. There's a mug of pink liquid, and two slices of something cake-like. I devour it all, savouring the tastes, still amazed at how satisfying this food is. I can almost feel it dissolving into me, feeding my mind and body, making me stronger.

The old man seems to be asleep, so I wait until I'm alone then try to get out of bed once more. The restraints don't give and I find there's something else I can't see holding me down. I slide myself underneath it. Amazingly, it seems to give . . . then a stabbing pain cuts through me. My ankle!

'Ouch!' I yelp.

The old man wakes and regards me with a level stare. 'You'd be better not try that,' he says. 'I'd have to call someone if you attempted to escape.'

I angrily pound my fist into the bed. It's not very satisfying when the soft covering absorbs the blow easily. 'Why? Why do you hate me?'

'I don't,' he replies regretfully. 'But I still have to do my duty.'

'Well, I hate you!' I burst out. 'I hate this stupid city! I want to go home!'

I turn away to face the window, seething.

Chapter 17
Arina

THEY come to examine me later that day, a whole procession of men and women, all in Guardian's robes. I concentrate on the colours of their sashes to keep my fear from spiralling out of control. Red is the highest rank; Arbitrators of Justice are the most highly-regarded of all Guardians. Purple is next, but if it's edged with yellow, it means the wearer has been assigned as an Overseer of a particular guild. Green and black are similar, but green has responsibilities as a Speaker, and can speak in the city's Court. There are a thousand other distinctions.

It's strange how important colours are in this world. I wonder if it has anything to do with how colourless the ice is? Or is it that the Sharian's skin and hair is so pale, so similar in tone, that they use the colours to help mark out their distinctions?

I know Rashae and Illortha, but the other four are strangers. And then another face appears. One that I recognise instantly.

It's Arina.

She's wearing her pale cream Novice robes and the same smug expression she had at Sarinne's house. She regards me coolly while I glare daggers at her.

They draw the filmy curtain aside and fan out around my bed. I try to imagine them as the crowd at a soccer game, but it's no use trying to calm myself with these thoughts. They're not cheering for me to score a goal. They're scrutinising me for very different reasons.

' . . . oddities with her colours,' one of them is saying, 'it might provide an explanation.'

Illortha shakes his head. 'I've never seen this kind of colouring . . . not on any human traveller I've examined.'

Arina speaks up. 'Guardians, with respect, could she be a half-breed? Her mother or father might be a traveller from our world.'

This possibility hasn't occurred to me. Could Mum be Sharian? No, definitely not. She's nothing like these people. But what about Dad? I doubted it. He's a big man, tall and dark-haired, not to mention bulky. Not at all like these Sharians.

Rashae silences her with a raised hand, and Arina takes a step back. She hangs her head but looks annoyed at being dismissed.

Rashae speaks. 'This is the reason I've called you here. We need to treat her. This, whatever it is that has allowed her to become so . . . close to being one of us, is preventing her recovery.

The examination should tell us more. We'll need to keep a close eye on her genetic markers and any other physiological similarities or differences, but also monitor her mental awareness. This should also tell us more.'

'How about telling *me* more?' I break in. 'How about telling me what's happening?'

Rashae's only answer is a command. 'Please hold still.'

As if I can do anything else.

They each place one hand on each other's shoulder. Some close their eyes, some tilt their heads back and all six of them take a deep, singular breath, and then . . . I *feel* it. I feel them dissecting me. They're looking closely at every square inch of my being. I think of science fiction TV shows where the hero has x-ray vision, able to see right through the skin to the skeleton. This is what they're doing to me, but closer, deeper, right down to a microscopic level.

'I can see it,' says Illortha. He sounds pleased. 'It's –'

'Of course. I should have seen it at once.' Rashae sounds relieved.

'What? What is it?' I'm begging them, hoping they'll answer me but knowing they won't. 'What's wrong with me?'

'We will have to remove it,' says one of the other Guardians.

'We'll do it immediately. The sooner this is corrected, the better.'

'I will inform the Healers,' says Illortha. 'Arina, you will attend. This will be your first surgical procedure?'

She looks up, and an excited expression crosses her face before she bows her head again.

'Hang on, you're not going to let her operate on me?' I can feel panic rising. I try to sit up but I can't move. I can't think how to get out from under the restraint. I struggle wildly. 'No way! She's too young! You can't do this! Let me go!'

I feel like I'm in a nightmare, the one where you're screaming and screaming and no sound is coming out. They all exit in single file, talking among themselves.

All except Arina. She hangs back as if she wants to approach but, at the same time, doesn't want to get too close.

'You tried to shame me,' she says at last. 'You know, this is a big opportunity for me. I haven't faced my Level Two examination yet, but they're giving me this opportunity because I did the right thing in telling them about you and the human boy. Why are you trying to ruin it?'

'Because, well, I'm not sure I trust you with a scalpel around me,' I laugh bitterly. 'You're not exactly my best friend, are you?'

She frowns. 'Why do you say that?'

'Just a feeling. You know, the whole demon thing.' I look at her more closely. I'm pretty sure she's sulking under the surface, and it makes me feel a bit kinder towards her. 'I'm sorry if we scared you.'

'You didn't *scare* me,' she says defiantly. 'But I'd never seen a human before. I was shocked.'

I lower my voice and nod towards the curtain and the other Healers. 'You know, I could tell them about the phone . . . the device you stole from me.'

Her eyes widen. I know she knows what I'm talking about. If the Guardians find out about her keeping the phone, she'll be facing the same punishment as Archon, even if she is in their good books for telling the Guardians about me and Daniel. She's clearly frightened by the thought, enough so that it breaks through her stony façade.

'Don't!' she begs me. 'Please don't. I didn't mean to take it. I found it next to you and I meant to look at it and give it to Mother. But then the voice spoke from the stone and I didn't want to give it up.'

'The voice?' I repeat. 'What voice?'

'It was a boy. He sounded nice. So I spoke to him. I said "Who are you?" and he heard me. He asked for you.'

Jake! I'd been talking to him as I crossed the bridge but I'd forgotten. Arina had said she'd heard someone speaking through the "demon-stone", but I'd been too wrapped up in what was happening to put the two facts together. It seems incredible that the phone call remained active through the barrier between our worlds.

If I call him back, dial his number, would it work? A phone call between worlds?

'When I said you were here, he sounded panicked. I said you were both okay. And then he told me that I have to help you.'

She looks at me evenly.

'I told him I can fix your leg. And that's what I'm going to do. I've been training for five years. Do you really think I can't do it, Keira?' Amazingly, she seems to be looking for my approval. Her eyes are cool, calm. 'You won't walk again if we don't treat you.'

I blink. 'So you're saying you can cure me.'

'The Healers think you have a chance.'

'A *chance?*'

'It's mostly because of the changes that are happening to you,' she tells me. 'They're speeding up. Your body is human and it's not made to handle this. Illortha said you won't survive if it keeps going. Rashae is worried too, but she's even more worried about what will happen to the balance of the worlds if it keeps going.'

'Oh, so this is about your precious balance. I should have known.' Just when I was starting to think someone actually cares about me! 'What are you going to do, amputate my leg?'

'Oh no,' she says, giving a tinkling laugh as if this should have been obvious. 'There's a bit of ice stuck in between the bones, like the blade of a knife that's snapped off at the handle.'

I don't like the sound of that. But how could a bit of ice have gotten stuck in my ankle?

'There was a snowstorm in my world. I was caught in it and I slipped. That's how I injured my ankle. But the doctors took heaps of x-rays and nothing showed up. They said they couldn't figure out why it wasn't healing properly.'

She looks away and nods, as if it were all making perfect sense to her.

'The ice is part of *our* world. The technology of your world might not show it. Even if it did, most people wouldn't know what it was. Humans don't know about the Ether, or the balance.'

'Some of them do,' I point out. 'Daniel knows about it. So does Jake.'

'Jake told me about the snowstorm,' Arina says. 'Not long ago there was an accident. Someone from Shar broke through the barrier between the worlds. That's probably what caused it.'

'Really?' I'm amazed. The cold snap we had definitely seemed weird. I hadn't realised *how* weird it was. I certainly hadn't thought it was caused by something in another world. 'How did it happen?'

'No one knows. At least, the Guardians won't tell us. But the piece of ice in your ankle is part of our world, and it wanted to come back. That's what made you come to our world. Illortha said it's giving you powers you should not have.'

'Who says I shouldn't have them?' I say incredulously. 'You? If all this is tied to the balance you keep talking about, then maybe this was all *supposed* to happen.'

She doesn't answer for a moment and I know I've got her stumped. Good.

'It doesn't change anything,' she says at last. 'We have to get it out or you'll never be able to use your leg properly. Either that, or the changes will kill you. The Guardians won't let the balance be upset in that way. And, even if it wasn't for all that, I told your friend I would help you. And I don't break my promises.'

Jake. She'd promised Jake she would help me. She'd actually spoken to him, had a conversation with him. My voice is strangled as I ask, 'So Jake knows I'm here? In Shar?'

'He knows more than most humans know about us. Talking to him was so fascinating! He told me not to tell the Guardians about the stone . . . the . . . the *phone*. I told him it was my duty. And then I meant to give the stone up to the Guardians but, by that time, it was too late. If I had come forward then I would have been punished.' She sounds like a real kid now. Like Daniel. She's clearly scared.

'Don't worry, I haven't told anyone you've got it. And I won't, as long as you bring it to me.'

'I can't do that,' she says.

'You can. Or I'll tell the Guardians that you've hidden technology from them.'

Her eyes fill with tears. I blink, surprised. Yep, they're real. The kid isn't a robot, after all!

I feel a little guilty. But not *very*.

The curtain whips back, and she looks over her shoulder at the Healers who are marching in to surround me. 'Okay,' she whispers. 'I'll do it.'

Chapter 18
The Surgery

THE Healers look eager, or as eager as any Sharian can look. I guess it must be exciting, performing surgery on someone from another world. I think of alien autopsy videos and nearly start giggling hysterically.

I find myself turning to Arina, feeling comforted by her presence. At least I think I can count on her now. She's showed her true self. I think she actually makes a really good Healer, or she will, when she's passed her Second Level exams. Would I trust her more, if she were twenty years older, or is that just my human view? If I'd grown up in Shar, I probably wouldn't think twice about having her here. Maybe it's just a human thing, my prejudice against her age. After all, there are plenty of smart kids back home; *I'm* smart, aren't I? But I can't vote yet, I don't have a say in who gets elected to run the government. I have to go to school. I can't just quit and play soccer. And that's what I'd do, if I had the choice. Why shouldn't I be allowed to do it? It's my own life.

Maybe we're the ones who've got it wrong.

'Are we prepared?' asks Illortha. There are nods and murmurs from the others.

I've only ever had one operation before, to get my wisdom teeth out. Mum paid extra for me to get it done in the chair, so I wouldn't have to get knocked out with an anaesthetic. So basically everything I know about surgery I learned from *Grey's Anatomy*.

Trust me, when you're lying on a bed on your back, unable to move, and you see those faces looking over you, it's a lot more scary than a TV show. You're putting your life in their hands. These people have power over you. They control your life . . . and your death.

And these people aren't even from my world. I wouldn't know if they were doing something wrong. And *they* might not even know!

' . . . carefully,' says one of the Healers. He tilts his head to one side. 'I'm probing at the edges. It seems to be melding with her tissues.'

'How is that possible?' asks another.

' . . . not certain . . . must be . . .'

Their voices lap over one another. They're all concentrating hard, moving their hands through the air, weaving invisible threads together. In and out, strengthening them with knots, making it solid and real, making it work.

This doesn't seem like a good idea. But, if it works, and they cure me, and I can walk again. Isn't that worth it? Of course . . . I'll never play soccer again anyway unless I can get back to my world. What would it matter if I could play or not, if I was marooned here?

' . . . need to separate . . .'

'I'm not seeing any division. Nothing to separate . . .'

I'd have to apply for a life task, wouldn't I? What would I *be*? I've never been any good at anything apart from soccer!

'It's working. Silence, now.'

Not to mention the one thing I can't change: the fact that I am human. Shar isn't exactly human-friendly, as Archon pointed out. The Guardians will probably lock me and Daniel up in a laboratory for study.

Or worse. They might think I'm too much of a risk. They might decide to get rid of us both!

If I didn't want to be pinned down to this bed before, well, I'm freaking out about it now. And that's when one of them says: 'It's free!'

Pulled back to reality, I realise that the Healers are moving away from one another. They all look exhausted. When I'd pushed away the restraining spell, I'd felt pretty tired so I guess what they're feeling is a hundred times worse.

One of them is holding something in his hands. It looks like a small piece of . . . well, ice.

It's small. Somehow, I thought it would be bigger because it caused me so much pain, but it's only the size of my index finger. And like Arina said, it's shaped like a knife.

I glance down at my leg. I'm still covered by the sheet. They didn't even remove it to do the operation. Wow.

So I guess there's no blood or gore. Not even any lingering pain, because whatever they've done is masking that too.

'I don't even get a cool scar?' I ask, pretending to be disappointed. None of them answers me, but I don't expect them to. I'm just relieved that it's over. And I'm still alive. 'Can I get out of this bed now?'

Illortha pulls back the curtain, exposing the room. The old man in the next bed blinks a few times, evidently waking from sleep. He speaks.

'Healer Hylbordan, I have a request for a slate and stylus. Might you also raise my pillows?'

With the excitement of the operation over business resumes as one of the Healers goes to help him, and Ilortha turns to answer my question.

'Not yet. You need to recover. Rest.'

'But I feel fine.'

'Novice Arina will be tending to you,' Illortha says. 'She will return once we're done with this briefing.'

The others are already leaving.

Chapter 19
Sharing Thoughts

A WAVE of sleepiness washes over me once I'm alone again. I feel like I've done eight soccer training sessions in a row. I guess the tiredness works both ways. The surgery has sapped my energy as well.

I fall deeply asleep. I don't even dream. When I wake up, I'm facing the old man opposite me who has, apparently, been watching me sleep.

'You look better,' he says. 'Less pale. More . . . human.'

'I feel better,' I say. It's true. I don't feel tired, spaced out, or sore. I feel *normal*. I haven't felt like this since before I broke my leg.

And then I realise . . . the colours are gone.

I can't see any aura around the old man at all.

He coughs . . . and keeps coughing. It's too deep, that cough. It sounds like it's ripping apart something inside him.

'Why aren't they treating you?' I ask.

'They are,' he says, genuinely surprised by the question.

'They're not doing anything.' These Healers can perform surgery without cutting skin, I'm pretty sure they can fix pneumonia or whatever he's got.

But he doesn't seem too concerned. 'I'm simply waiting for my appointment.'

'An appointment for what?'

'*Valatha*. My death.' He states blankly, as if he doesn't care. And, looking at him, I don't think he does at all. There's no hidden fear or sorrow in his eyes.

'You . . . what? You're given a *time* to die?'

He responds in the same calm, neutral voice. 'It's only natural. A bed is allocated to each of us when we apply for our time.'

'*Natural?*' My voice rises in pitch and the rest comes out as a screech. 'But it's . . . it's not . . . that's barbaric!' I remember studying euthanasia in school. Mrs Hayes explained how it was acceptable in a few cultures but illegal in most.

'And your way isn't?' the old man sighs. 'You fight to keep people alive, prolonging their pain if they are ill or injured, and drawing out the process as their body gradually shuts down. Sometimes you keep them alive using machines, even for years at a time. As a Guardian working for the Guild of Overseers I reached Tenth Level. I was allowed to glimpse your world, and I know what happens there.'

I gape at him. What astounds me is not what he's talking about, allowing people to die at a time of their choosing is not news to me, it's in the media all the time. It's that I can't disagree with him and that forms a cold, hard knot in my chest.

He's right about accepting death; it's something every person has to understand – that sooner or later everyone dies. But aren't we supposed to fight to stay alive? Every instinct we've got is coded for survival, to keep us living and breathing for as long as possible. Choosing to die would be admitting defeat. And *letting* someone choose to die means you don't care about them.

But then . . . how can I judge this man, whose name I don't even know, for his decision? I mean, if I was old and facing months or years of sickness, maybe *I'd* want to have that option.

I think of Jake's mum and the pain she endured in her last months. The chemotherapy and drugs . . . how she lost her memory and patches of her hair and some of her teeth. She lost all her strength and couldn't walk, not even with help, or do regular *mum* things for Jake and Daniel. 'Does everyone do this . . . *valatha* thing?' I ask.

'We all know when it's time to apply for admission to the Healers Hall. The balance calls us. We don't fear death or try to keep it at bay like you humans do, Keira. We Sharians recognise our place in the universe.'

I roll onto my back and look up at the ceiling. It's pure white, spotless. I don't know what to feel. I've been so angry with the Guardians for looking down on my world as savage and primitive. But maybe we do have it wrong . . . about some things, anyway.

'So you're all just like "I've lived a good life, that's it"?'

He smiles. 'It's true, I have lived a productive and useful life. I'm happy with what I've accomplished, and others are also satisfied with what I've done. I've left behind a good record.'

Records again. 'What's the deal with records?' I ask. 'Everyone's so worried about them. What are they? Why do they matter so much?'

'A record is a registration of your name and your achievements, good and bad. They are stored in crystals in the Hall of Records. Anyone can access these throughout your life and, once you have gone through *valatha*, they are stored in archives. That way nothing is lost. Leaving behind a good record is everyone's greatest desire.'

'What will be in your record?' I'm curious. 'What does an Overseer do?'

'Many things.' He seems pleased with this question and I wonder if he's been lonely in here by himself. He obviously likes to talk, and I doubt the Healers are very good listeners.

'We are assigned to look after the working of the major institutions: the Etherium, the

Libraries and Archives, the outer healing centres, the Social Quarters and the Production sectors. Of course, there are those who work here in the Chambers with the judges, record-keepers, and Healers. There are some who work with the Ministers, who provide guidance in the ways of the Ether, and they conduct the Rituals or birth and death. There are those who work with the Officials, who monitor their work and regulate trade between the industries and the public. There is also a Guild of Overseers who check the streets and buildings to ensure they are kept healthy and safe.

'I worked with the department that deals with Forbidden Objects. If a person was suspected of having or creating something that breaches the Edict in its design or function, it was my job to track them down.'

He smiles sadly, as if a painful memory is linked with this.

'I'm guessing it wasn't always fun and games.'

'I did my job well. A little too well.' He sighs again, and it rattles in his chest and makes him cough. 'They said you have the ability to use the *ilhwarh*.'

I nod. 'Yeah. Well, at least, that I can use it. But maybe not, now that the shard is gone. I can't see your aura anymore.'

He wriggles a bit in his bed and reaches across the space between us. Opening his fist, he reveals the knife-shaped shard they pulled out of my ankle.

'How did you get that?' I ask, gaping at him.

He makes a movement that might be a shrug and it sets him coughing again. Of course! He must have done it when he'd called the Healer over to him after my surgery. Somehow he'd picked his pocket. But why? If he's so concerned with his record, why would he want to break the rules?

'They would have locked it up,' he says. 'They would have examined it then made sure it was broken down and destroyed. But I think you were meant to have this. I think it was meant to come to you. And there's something I need tell you . . . this shard will help me do that. Can you reach it?'

I stretch as far as I can, feeling the restraint tugging me back as I do so, but I manage to touch his fingers. They're ice cold. I shiver. I don't think they'd have felt that cold if I still had the shard inside me.

As I wrap my fingers around the shard, my fingers brush his hand and I feel something leap inside me, just like when Archon had touched me. The images come quickly but they're blurred at the edges, muffled. I can't feel and smell them. It's more like watching a TV through a shop window, the sound is muted and the images are half-hidden by reflections. The shard is sharing them with me, as it was before, but I'm no longer part Sharian, no longer able to experience the full thing.

. . . I'm standing in a room with a tiled floor and wide windows. A man and a woman are standing in front of me. She is beautiful, more beautiful than any other woman I've ever seen. I take a deep breath, awed to be in the same space as such perfection.

'Guardian Laith,' says the man. 'This is Thandera. You will be working with her as your partner from now on . . .'

I am awed by the honour.

In my mind, I see years pass in a blur of movement and feeling.

I stand beside Thandera in front of a room full of people, making a speech. I walk with her along a path overlooking the vinarhi, the mist-water, and we both look up at the permanently twilit sky. I hold her hand as she recites the words of joining at our Ceremony, 'I promise to be with you for all time, to love and hold you dear to me, to be your guide and follower. This is my oath.'

I feel a warm glow of happiness spread through me.

There is a sudden jerk and *I am looking down at a slate of thin crystal. There are words skating over its surface. It is a missive from the Council.*

'. . . an incursion into the Forbidden Objects repository. The items listed as missing are these: two semi-cubits of brass-metal, four semi-cubits of copper-metal, three sections of a sub-stance known only as "glass". All are high-level

and have dangerous applications. Most urgent. You are called to service.

I knew this meant that I, the part of me that was living these memories as the old man, would not be able to return home until the case was solved. This was a vital mission.

Again, I skipped through time. Now *I'm climbing a narrow stairway behind another man in Guardian's robes, who is speaking to me over his shoulder.*

'The disturbance was only noted because of a random check. This building hasn't been assessed in years.'

'I can tell,' I say, looking at the dull and darkened walls. They are fractured in places, completely blackened in others by large black spots, like mould.

We come to a door and he pushes it open. In-side is a cluster of tables and benches covered in many different objects. I step closer to examine them, careful not to disturb anything. They are forbidden things and, as Keira, I recognise them: a Bunsen burner connected to a small tank of gas, a pair of metal tongs, a kiln the size of a small safe, rasps, files and metal-cutters.

'From the look of them,' I say, as I finish my examination. 'These objects have been used to melt the metal and smelt the glass. The stolen substances have been altered by their contact with heat. Remade.'

'Which explains why we can't locate them through etheric means.'

I felt his desperation and utter despair. It had been a month since he had seen his home and his precious Thandera. This last clue seemed like just another dead end.

And then . . .

. . . I wake from my sleep to a ringing noise. A transmission, coming through my crystal receiver.

I look across to a table beside my bed, where a small tablet sits, like the one the girl Healer was holding earlier. It's pulsing with light and giving out a ringing sound. I know this means it's an urgent transmission.

And —

I'm walking briskly, trying not to break into a run. I am in the Chambers, hurrying across the atrium. I burst through a huge doorway into the grand court room. Such a huge room! It's like a great cavern, ringed with seats and delicate, decorative pillars. Many of the seats are filled with city-dwellers. In the centre is a circular space like a stage. There are flickering lights on pedestals. No, they're not lights, they're flames. Blue flames that burn without fuel. Inside this ring is a raised dais of rock-crystal.

The dais is divided into separate tiers, with seats arranged at various levels. At the top is a chair that looks a lot like a throne. In this sits a woman in Guardian's robes and I know this is the Chief Arbitrator, Iranth. In the tiers below her sit the Council members and judges.

The flickering light makes it seem like the separate sections are spinning in different directions. It's unnerving. I think it's meant to give the impression of grandeur as, positioned at the very base, there is a smaller dais where the accused is supposed to sit. They can't look behind them to see the proceedings. They face outwards, towards the audience.

And there is Thandera, sitting in that seat, her face carefully neutral.

'. . . *to the charge of theft and to the charge of using forbidden materials, to the charge of hiding your crime from the Guardians and the law, to the charge of creating something dangerous and forbidden, you are judged guilty –*'

'No!' I yell.

Is it me, Keira, or the old man who says this? Maybe both of us. I find I've got tears in my eyes as I realise how that woman betrayed him, and his entire world, by doing something so stupid.

And the Chief Arbitrator rises from her chair and raises something above her head.

In her hands is the telescope.

I know it's my telescope. Jake's telescope. *The* telescope. It's shiny and new, but the same one. I'd know it anywhere. And she made it. Thandera.

It all makes sense.

The old man is looking at me. I've let go of his hand.

'I know her,' I say. 'I've seen her. But not here . . . in my world.'

'I know,' he says sadly. 'I saw it in your thoughts. I was hoping . . . I always hoped that she still lived, and that she was happy.'

'I think she is.' I don't think that's a lie, even though I've never once seen Mrs Henders crack a smile. I feel a twinge of guilt though; when I remember Jake told me Mrs Henders had been married once. I never guessed it was in another world. I search for something I can tell him, some news I can offer that might comfort him. 'She, um, has a lot of lawn ornaments.'

He lies back in his bed with a sigh.

'She always loved your world. When she was exiled, I often wondered if that was what she always wanted. If I wasn't enough of a reason for her to stay here . . .'

'There are different reasons why people do things.' I think about why I stole the telescope . . . my burning desire to *know* what it was. 'She probably couldn't help herself.'

'Please, will you take my hand once more?'

I do so, securing my hand in his, the shard between us.

I'm watching as Thandera/Mrs Henders is led up the steps from the centre of the Court Hall. I push forwards, anxious, and desperate. They can't take her away from me! They can't banish her! And all of a sudden, we're face-to-face.

'Why did you do this?' I beg her.

'I wanted to see, wanted to know.' She isn't crying. She isn't scared. She's angry. 'I wanted

to let them know, those people in the Below World, that the Guardians want something from them. Something is going to happen, Laith. We're building towards it. I thought I could make a difference.'

I'm confused and frightened. But they're pulling her away. Too late . . .

'What did she think was going to happen?' I ask.

'Thandera always saw things that I didn't,' he answers. 'But sometimes I wondered if some of it was mere fantasy. This, what she spoke of, didn't make any sense. But I began to wonder, nevertheless. And, the more I thought about it, the more I heard and saw. Whispers. Hushed conversations. Documents and references . . . things that pointed out how much the Guardians know of the Below World and the effort they're making to gather more knowledge.'

'But they hate the Below World,' I say. 'Why would they want to collect information about it?' And then I think, and it's a scary thought, why does anyone want to know everything about a place? So they can find their way around it. Know what to expect when they get there.

It feels like something cold and dark is crawling around in my chest.

'Fear makes people do strange things. I think what Thandera meant was for me to challenge what I believed. And for the first time, I did. I started to ask questions. And I hated what I learned . . . there are things about Shar that are buried deep because they are ugly and unwelcome. The Guardians tell us to strive and work hard and disdain unworthy thoughts and emotions – fear, jealousy, hatred – but these things are still there. Hidden.

'And when people fear something as much as the Guardians fear the Below World, they do things that might go against their beliefs. They might think they're doing it for the right reasons; to protect others and keep themselves safe.

'But they're *afraid*. They watch what's happening to your world. They've seen the poisons choking your skies, the natural cycles failing, and the balance being torn apart. What will happen when it's finally gone?'

'That's crazy!' I laugh incredulously. 'That's insane. Earth can't just *die*. It's –'

'Please,' he stops me by raising a hand. 'There's not much time, and I have more to show you.'

I'm walking down the aisle between towering walls. Alcoves have been carved into them and are filled with more objects I recognise. Toasters, Buddha statues, CDs, folded raincoats, mismatched Converse shoes, old Gameboys and lipsticks . . . all things from my world. Things that might be carried in the pockets of people like me, who stumble into Shar by accident.

I stop before a particular section. I'm looking for something. But it's clearly missing and the assigned alcove is empty. Puzzled, I look around.

Again, another shift in space and time.

I'm looking down at a man sitting behind a desk. He's working on something, clearly not paying much attention.

'But I don't understand.' I say. 'I placed the telescope in the archives myself.'

'Those objects have been listed as removed.' The man says. 'They've been relocated to the Etherium for study. I'm sorry. I can't grant you access.'

'No one is supposed to study Forbidden Objects,' the old man's voice broke through the memory. 'That was my job; to classify them, and set them aside. To protect them. So I was intrigued, and I looked further. I found out where the telescope was being kept. I broke some of the rules to get inside. And what I found when I did . . .'

My heart is racing. I'm in a long room. In the centre is a clear crystal case. The rest of the room is lined with benches. On the benches are tools. Materials. Glinting metals, sheets of glass. Some are cut into various shapes while others are twisted and half put together. There's no one else here, but I feel like I'm being watched . . . still, I take a step forwards.

Mounted in the case in the centre of the room is Thandera's telescope.

Most of the objects in this room, I realise, are telescopes of different shapes and sizes.

Without a second thought, I race across the room, my feet skidding on the floor. I reach into the crystal case. I grab Thandera's telescope. And I run.

And then I see . . .

. . . a bridge. It's shining, golden and beautiful. I'm standing there, watching as a group of men and women in Guardian's robes lead Thandera forwards.

'We sentence you to banishment for your crimes,' says one of them. It's Chief Arbitrator Iranth. 'You will never return to Shar.'

I step forwards. The Guardians holding her step aside, giving me the moment I need. I reach for her elbow and grip it briefly, letting the ihlwarh flow between us. 'I will miss you,' I say. And I slip the telescope into her sleeve.

She nods, and they motion her forwards once more.

It's the last time I see her. She vanishes with the telescope she made and the secret of its purpose.

'I couldn't let them have it,' he says. 'That secret. It felt too wrong. By giving it to her, I removed the threat from Shar. I did my duty.'

'You broke the rules!' I've been thinking of him as a straight-laced, law-abiding citizen. I'm glad to realise he's not – I like him a lot more now! 'But why were they making all those telescopes? You don't think the Guardians would do something like . . . I don't know, invade the Below World?'

It sounds crazy. But . . .

'I don't know what they mean to do. They fear that your people, if they knew about Shar, would not hesitate to take it for themselves.'

'Oh, so that makes it all right for them to try and destroy us?'

He shakes his head. 'I needed to share this with you. The secret will die with me, otherwise. You might want to keep this,' he says, tossing the shard to me. 'A memento of your experience.'

'Yeah. A souvenir.'

I tuck it under my pillow, thinking: a souvenir only becomes a souvenir after you get home.

***

They come for him later that night. It happens quickly and efficiently.

Jake told me his mum took hours to die. He wasn't there when it finally happened because his dad sent him home to sleep. He always said he wished he'd been there, so that he'd been able to say goodbye properly, but he reckoned she probably wouldn't have been able to hear him anyway. She was kind of drifting by then.

But this . . . this was timed perfectly. The Healers gather around the bed and another Guardian in pure white robes arrives to confer softly with them.

Three other people enter the Sanatorium; two men and a young woman that the old man,

Laith, seems to recognise. They greet him and the woman bends over to embrace him.

'I will miss you,' she says in a half-whisper, tears in her voice.

'And I you, granddaughter,' he replies. 'You look more like your mother every day. Be obedient and steadfast. I know you will do well.'

She straightens. 'Of course I will.'

'It is time,' says one of the Healers, gently ushering her aside. I recognise the white-robed Guardian from the borrowed memories of the crystal shard. He is the Minister of Rites. He places his hands on either side of the Laith's face and gently slows his breathing to match Laith's.

Under the pillow, I reach for the shard. Holding it tightly, the colours return. I can faintly see his aura. It's blue. A calm blue. But it's . . . I don't know how to describe it . . . loose, I guess. There are wisps and tendrils coming off it.

'You have proved your worth, Laith. Your essence will return to the Ether as the cycle continues. May you find peace there as you have here.'

He releases his hold and there is a moment where everything becomes silent and still. Then Laith's blue aura begins to drift and fade, like smoke from a doused fire, until I can't see it anymore.

He's gone.

The woman gives a muffled sob and the man quickly touches her arm. The Minister nods towards the door and leads them out of the room.

The Healers gather close.

'The seed crystal?' asks one of them and he is handed a small green rock. He presses this onto Laith's chest, just above where a human heart would be. The crystal glows slightly, and then brightens. It's growing, spreading out crackling little vines that wrap around his body until he's completely covered. Then, when the light becomes so bright I think it'll blind us all, it starts to fade and disappears altogether. And there's nothing left behind. No trace of Laith at all.

Chapter 20
Walking

I CAN'T keep from touching the shard under my pillow.

If it's true and the old man has joined the Ether, then he must still be here in some form. If the Sharians are right and there really is such a thing as immortality, then perhaps death isn't something to fear, or fight against, after all.

I wonder if the Ether exists for humans as well.

My thoughts are interrupted by someone coming into the room. I'm both glad and anxious to see its Arina.

She looks a lot less sure of herself than the last time I saw her as she glances around the empty Sanatorium. The room feels terribly big now that Laith is gone and Arina looks tiny as she walks towards me.

She stops, her hands hanging loosely by her sides, and looks at me.

'I brought your stone,' she says.

'It's called a phone,' I say with a grin. 'Hand it over.'

She hesitates, chewing her lower lip, then reaches into her robes and pulls out my phone. I'm so glad to see it, but it suddenly looks strange in this place, as if it's not quite real. The colour is too bright. The clean, shiny plastic cover doesn't fit in here.

I take it and flip it open. Surely it can't be . . . but it is. It's still charged.

Arina is staring at me. 'How do you make it talk?'

I hit the recent calls key. Jake's number pops up instantly. I hit the green call button and hold my breath.

Nothing.

No dial tone, no busy signal.

'Isn't it working?' Arina sounds let down, it's not fair that she's disappointed. I'm the one whose future is on the line here!

'Damn it!' I say, slamming the phone down on the bed.

'Is it broken? Maybe you can fix it –'

'No, I can't *fix* it,' I inform her angrily. 'I don't know how –' My voice cracks as the tears break through. I sob loudly. The phone was my last hope. What am I going to do now?

'I'm sorry,' she says in a quiet little voice. 'I didn't mean for this to happen. I should have realised the balance can't be tipped. When I stole from you I took something I wasn't meant to. Now Archon is paying for it. But maybe I can make it up.' She looks at me hopefully. 'Can I? Can I do something for you?'

'Not unless you can build a bridge between this world and my home,' I say. 'That's all I want. I wish I'd never gone out in that stupid storm! I never would have broken my leg. I never would have started to change, I wouldn't have stolen the telescope from Jake, and I never would have ended up here!'

'But Shar is nicer than your world.' She says this as if she genuinely believes it, like she doesn't understand why I'm upset at all.

I stare at her. Just like I how I compared the scent of *vinarhi* to violets, because I could on compare it to something I already knew, Arina can't see beyond what she's familiar with. I can't blame her for that.

'Shar is pretty incredible, but it's not my home. I've got school . . . I'm missing classes and soccer practice.' Now I've started, I can't stop the words pouring out of my mouth. 'There's my mum . . . and my friends and my dog . . . but you don't even know what a dog is, do you?'

'No, but –'

'Then don't just assume your world is better than mine, okay?! There are good things about the Below World too. There are people there that I really care about.'

'The Guardians always tell us the Below World is a bad place.'

'Well, at least we don't send people to jail just for *helping* someone! Archon didn't do anything wrong.'

'He made a mistake. But they'll let him go.'

'Are you sure?' I ask, because I'm really not. 'From the sounds of things, he might be facing serious punishment.'

She looks at me, worry in her eyes. 'I wish I hadn't told them,' she whispers.

I shrug. 'But you did.'

'I really miss him,' she says, looking downcast.

I stare at her. This is a different person, someone who cares about her brother. It's nice to see.

'Can I keep this?' she asks, and I see she's holding my phone. I nod. She might as well. It's useless now.

***

That afternoon, I'm allowed to take a walk.

'Your leg needs movement to build muscle back up,' explains Illortha, as if this is something beyond my understanding. 'Keeping yourself active is the best cure.'

'How about you remove the restraining charm permanently?' I say in what I hope is a coaxing voice. 'I promise you I'll stay as active as I can.'

He ignores me. 'I've removed as much of the pain as possible.'

I've spent most of the past few days flat on my back. Moving is such a relief! I slide off the bed, careful to keep my weight on my hands until I'm sure my leg can take it. And it can.

'Can you take one step?' asks Illortha.

I oblige him. I'm stiff and achy in places, and it feels like I'm heavier than I used to be, but I take a careful step. Then another.

Standing there without my crutches, I want to perform some stretches, practise some kicks. I want to run. I could run, couldn't I? Bolt out the door and just race out into the city?

But where would I go? Sarinne's house would be the first place they'd look, and I'm not sure I could find my way back there. Besides, there's no telling how long this pain relief stuff will last. I'd probably get out the front door and collapse . . .

And then there's Daniel. Unless they've moved him since they bought him in with Archon, he's still here in the Chambers somewhere and I can't leave without him.

And I don't want to leave without seeing Archon again. Without thanking him for trying to keep us safe from the Guardians. I owe him that. At least, that's what I try to tell myself. But there's *something* that's been niggling at the back of my mind . . . how I feel about him . . . which is just crazy! I mean, he's from another world. He probably doesn't think of me like that. And *I* definitely shouldn't be thinking of him like that.

Illortha gets me to walk from one end of the room to the other, then back again. By that time I'm buggered, and I've got proof that I'm not running anywhere anytime soon.

Illortha speaks to another Healer as I climb back into bed. I listen closely, wondering if these two are part of the group that Laith had mentioned. I can't imagine them planning and scheming about anything. They're so calm and collected. But maybe it's exactly *that*, their coldness and distance that I need to worry about.

'. . . there are significant changes in her aura. She is anxious about something, and it is affecting the healing. It might take longer than we imagine.'

'It does not matter. She can be treated in the cells just as well as here.'

I suppose I knew they would lock me away. But, although I've been waiting for it, my mouth goes dry at the thought. 'You're putting me in jail?'

They turn to look at me. I hold my breath, worried they can feel what I'm thinking. Now that the shard is gone, I can't use the *ihlwarh* anymore. Surely they can't read my mind?

'Your trial has been scheduled for tomorrow.' Illortha informs me. 'Along with your companion.'

'Trial?' I squeak, my stomach filling with cold dread.

***

Arina returns later in the afternoon, but now that Illortha is here, she's quiet. She's carrying a tray of food. It tastes different now that the shard has been removed from my ankle. Bland and insubstantial. I wonder if I'll get used to it, or if now I'm back to being human I'll start craving macaroni cheese again.

Arina looks away when I try to meet her gaze.

'I'm sorry,' she whispers. 'I tried to get them to keep you in here, but they wouldn't.'

'It doesn't make a difference where I'm locked up,' I tell her, even though it kind of does. I've never been to prison before, not even on a school excursion. I guess the upside is I can boast to my mates that I've served time before I even turned sixteen. If only I *wanted* to boast about something like that . . .'

'I'll do what I can,' she says but by then, Illortha is back and Arina is ordered to report to her work station while I rest.

'I'm sick of resting,' I grouch, but two minutes later I'm out like a light.

Chapter 21
The Trial

THEY come to get me the next day. It's evening. The only way to tell the passage of time is when the lights dim. Outside the window, nothing changes except for the wheeling of the stars and the glittering patches of shifting lights on my world overhead.

Moments earlier, I'd pulled out the crystal shard. I know I can't leave it here. I don't want them to figure out it was Laith who pinched it for me. He deserves to keep his spotless record.

So I tuck it into my robe and tighten my sash to keep it in place. I finish making my adjustments just as Guardian Rashae strides into the room.

'Remove her restraints,' she orders.

Illortha does so. I find it easier to slip off the bed this time. I'm still stiff, but it's less like I'm trying to move through water. I also feel a lot stronger.

Apart from Rashae and Illortha, there are four others who take up position around me. As we make our way slowly through the passages and up the stairs, it becomes clear that things are different this time. My honour guard isn't just trying to keep me from bolting but is also trying to shield me.

There are people in the passageway and on the stairs. Despite the Guardians trying to keep my presence a secret, word has leaked out about what I am, and all of them are looking at me with obvious interest. Above us, people are leaning over their balconies to get a better view, pretending, of course, that they're just taking a break from work or their daily errands.

And I'm guessing my changes must be reversing because I hear snatches of their whispered conversations.

'Look at her hair,' I hear one of them say. 'So much colour!'

I always hated my hair. Now I hate it even more as it marks me as an outsider in Shar.

The Guardians are busy glaring and looking official, trying to intimidate everyone into ignoring me but it's not easy. You can't stop people gawking at a spectacle.

'This is unacceptable,' hisses Rashae under her breath. 'I asked for all non-essential workers to be kept out of this area. It's closing time, they should be in their homes.'

'They did their best, but the Council feels there is more harm in keeping people from performing their daily tasks than in keeping this secret from them. That's also why they refused a closed trial.'

She huffs angrily. 'This will only feed the rumours.'

'There are enough rumours already,' Illortha replies. 'They feel *some* information is better than none.'

'Pssh! What they want is another example. They want to parade the human they've caught in front of the whole city so they'll be seen as the heroes who saved Shar from invasion once more.'

We reach the top of the stairs and cross a wide atrium.

There are even more people here. They jostle and push to get a view, but not like the way a soccer crowd does. It's more like the crowd in a museum, with everyone politely not trying to get in anyone else's way, while still getting a good view of the exhibit.

The crowd parts in front of us, showing a huge pair of doors. These fold back on themselves as we approach, revealing an enormous room.

It's the same chamber I saw in Laith's memory, the courtroom where Thandera AKA Mrs Henders was tried and sentenced. It's different now I'm seeing it in person. Bigger, and far more frightening.

Steps lead down through the seats to the central ring. The seats are filling up as we come in, and from what I can see, it's going to be a full house.

My heart starts to race but there's no backing out of this. The Guardians aren't letting me move anywhere but forwards. Without touching me, they shepherd me ahead, down to the central tiers. We pass between the pillars, and walk between the pedestals with their flickering blue flames. The whirling designs of the tiers have a hypnotic effect. I almost lose my balance as Rashae urges me to climb to the next level.

She pushes me into a seat, and I look out at the crowd. I'm sitting in the chair where Thandera sat at her trial.

Rashae takes a seat beside me. 'Say nothing unless you're asked to,' she says in a clipped voice. 'Answer truthfully. And politely,' she adds, and I decide then and there that I'll be my usual blunt, straightforward self.

There is a wave of murmuring and someone else is led through the door. My heart leaps. Daniel! I drink in the sight of him, unable to believe he's safe and alive. He looks tired and his hair is a mess, but other than that, he seems fine. They lead him down towards the dais and into a seat below me.

'Daniel!' I shout, not caring that my voice sounds louder than it should in this room. 'Daniel!'

He turns around and looks up at me. I can see the fear in his eyes but he raises his hand and gives a little wave. That familiar gesture is so much like the Daniel I've always known that I almost laugh with relief.

'Quiet,' Rashae orders.

Despite the amount of people, everything happens in an orderly fashion. Everyone takes their seats. A woman comes in through the main door and I can tell she's someone important. The clamour of movement and soft, chattering voices dies.

I recognise her now. She's Chief Arbitrator Iranth, the one who sentenced Thandera. She's wearing her bright red sash, she resembles the rest of the Sharians with her pale skin, pure white hair and blue eyes. She doesn't look at me but I've never seen anyone, not even Rashae, with such cold eyes. Her demeanour reminds me of the judges on Earth; someone who is used to being listened to. She walks down the steps and climbs the central tiers; as she passes my bay, I can feel her gaze pass over me. She's not pleased with what she sees. I don't need to see her aura to know that.

Reaching the top she turns to addresses the room. 'We are gathered here,' she says, 'to witness the judgement on the fate of this human.'

With one voice, everyone replies with what I guess this is the expected response. 'We gather in this Hall to witness the justice of the Council.'

'The human Keira and the human Daniel have entered our world,' Iranth continues. Her voice is loud and strong, ringing through the courtroom which I suspect was probably designed to carry sound. 'The balance called the girl Keira, for she carried within her a fragment of our world, which needed to be returned. Now it has been done. Her fate, and the fate of her companion, is to be decided.'

I guess this is as good a time as any to start causing a ruckus. 'If it's all about the balance,' I say, 'then you need to send both of us back.'

'Silence!' The Chief Arbitrator bellows and the sound reverberates across the courtroom. She's furious. 'You will *not* speak, human.'

She pauses a moment while the echoes fade, then continues. 'You are correct that the balance needs to be restored. You, and your companion, have no place here.

'We all know what humans have done to their world. They've poisoned their air and waterways. They've stripped their land. They've exploited and neglected their own people. They have twisted and formed dirty devices out of the resources of their planet, which they have then used to do more damage. Can we allow one of them among us?'

'You're wrong!' I burst out, craning my head back to see her. 'You've never been to the Below World; to Earth. You don't know anything about us!'

'Do you deny that humans do these things?' she asks coldly.

'No,' I say. 'No, we do some pretty horrible stuff . . . but we do good things, too. We make things . . . we build houses and hospitals, we create things like art and poetry and . . . and

. . . we have good things like ice-cream and friends and soccer . . . and . . .

'And there are people, really good people, who spend their lives helping others, like my friend Mikhal's parents. They're solicitors, and they help accident victims and people who've been injured, and try to make up for things they've lost. And what about my mum?. She works like crazy so I can go to school and we can have a house and a car and . . . and so that she can make things better for us, for me.'

'My stepmum tries to help people too,' Daniel adds. 'She works with charities and poor people. She doesn't get anything out of it for herself. You can't blame all of us for what a few people do.'

Iranth's voice doesn't soften. 'Yet we all suffer the consequences of any negative actions. We must do what we can to contain the effects. Thus, I impose the sentence of enforced *valatha*.'

'*What?*' I yelp. Even the crowd is shocked. You can hear the gasps and murmurs. I know this must be unusual. Even the criminals Archon mentioned, who get chucked in the cells, get to decide whether they apply for *valatha* or not. Panic rushes through me. I look frantically at Daniel and, although he probably doesn't know what *valatha* is, he sees how horrified I am and shrinks back in confusion and terror.

'No! You can't do that! It's . . . that's barbaric!'

'SILENCE! I will not tolerate any more of

this. Take her to the cells.'

'No!' I yell. 'I'll say what I like, you old bag! This world could use a bit more honesty. You're always hiding things from everyone and telling them what to think. Maybe you're all happy with that.' I stand up and face the crowd. They're even more shocked now that I would dare speak out. 'Well, stuff you all! If you're so concerned with what's happening on Earth, why don't you help us? Why don't you share your magic and healing powers with us instead of sitting up here thinking you're better than everyone else? You don't even see what's happening! You don't know how much your precious Guardians are hiding from you! They've got *technology* –'

'Take her away,' Guardian Iranth says. 'Quickly!'

Rashae yanks my arms behind me, pulling me back. It's the first time she's touched me but she doesn't seem concerned about how "dirty" I am now. She manhandles me out of the stand and onto the steps. I try to wrench myself away, searching frantically for Daniel in the crowd.

'Move,' Rashae hisses in my ear, pushing me down the steps towards the door. The crowd parts around me, backing away from us with a mixture of fear and fascination.

And then suddenly I'm outside.

The cool air fills my lungs. It's refreshing and I take deep breaths, starting to come back to myself.

Illortha peers into my eyes. 'Are you well?' he asks. 'Can you speak?'

'I'm . . . fine,' I gasp out.

'I'm sorry,' he says. 'I've been denied permission to return you to the Sanatorium.'

I don't care about that right now. 'Where's Daniel?'

He shakes his head and I look around wildly.

People are starting to come out of the Court. They mill around, staring at me and I inhale deeply.

'Daniel!' I yell.

But whatever they're planning to do with me, they're going to do with doing him as well. He emerges in the midst of three tall Guardians, looking pale.

When he sees me, words tumble out of him. 'I'm so glad you're okay! They fixed your leg. How did they do that? You are okay, aren't you?'

'I'm fine. But what about you? How did they catch you?'

He shrugs, looking slightly embarrassed. 'I went looking for you.'

'You idiot!' I say, but without anger. I'm not mad at him. Actually, I'm kind of glad he's here and not wandering around out there in the city alone. 'You should have stayed where you were.'

'I saw the Guardians arrive. I stayed where I was while they went in, but then I saw them come out with you and I knew they'd come looking for me next. I thought if I could get to Archon, he could help me. I was trying to break through the spell on the door when the Guardians came out. I tried to run and I kicked one of them . . . but they put some kind of spell on me. I could walk, but only in the direction they wanted me to. I saw Archon. They arrested him, too, Keira.'

'I know. Did you see where he was taken?'

'No. They wouldn't let me talk to him. They took me to a room and locked me in. It was all white crystal, and I couldn't even find the door when it was closed. I was . . . pretty scared.' He says this hesitantly, obviously thinking he sounds like a wuss.

I want to tell him it's okay and everything will be fine, but I can't lie to him, so I just give him a quick hug before we're ushered through a small side door which closes behind us, blocking out the noise of the crowd. We're led to a desk where a young man sits. He gets out of his seat, a stool made of white soft-looking material, the moment he sees us and picks up a small rectangular crystal. He stands hesitantly in front of me.

'Check her!' says Rashae sharply.

He holds the crystal in front of me and waves it up and down.

Rashae sees my look of alarm and misinterprets it. 'No one is granted access to the cells below without being checked for forbidden items.'

Just like a security wand at an airport, and I've got the crystal shard. Its jabbing into my waist and I'm sure he's going to find it now but then he puts the wand aside.

'She's clean.'

Amazed, I look down at the sash which hides the crystal at my waist. I don't know why he didn't pick up the shard, unless it was because it was once a part of me. Maybe it still is and that means I'll always be part Sharian, too.

Daniel is treated to the same examination, and then the young man takes another crystal. This he fits into the wall behind him and a door slides smoothly open, revealing a long narrow corridor of rock-crystal.

There's something different about this crystal, though. It looks harder and sharper but also duller and more metallic. I'm relieved to be away from the scrutiny of all those people, but I can feel a chill in the air. This is not a place anyone wants to go.

I hesitate. Suspecting that I'm about to run the Guardians tense around me, but it's Rashae who speaks.

'You should not have called the Guardians into question, Keira. Chief Arbitrator Iranth is a powerful woman. She's not someone you want as an enemy.'

'So what?' I return, despair in my voice. 'You all think we're your enemies anyway. You decided that before you even met me!' An idea hits me and I narrow my eyes. 'You know about it, don't you? What they plan to do to my world. You're part of it.'

She regards me evenly, refusing to answer my question.

Compared to Iranth's harsh voice, Rashae's silence is far scarier.

Chapter 22
Beneath the Chambers

WE WALK for minutes through sharp angled corridors and down numerous steps. It seems to get darker as we descend. The walls are less well-formed, less regular and geometrical, more like the walls of caves. They don't glow like the other rock-crystal walls. Instead, there are illuminated globes placed at intervals. I have a feeling we're below the level of the building, deep inside the foundations of this world, what Rashae had called the *hallichar*. These hallways might not have been grown at all, but created by whatever natural forces formed this world.

We come to a hatch in the floor, a dark circle of metal-like material. The young man bends and picks up a small, ancient-looking padlock, the kind that's heart-shaped with a keyhole in the front. He pulls a heavy old-fashioned key from around his neck and unlocks it, sliding it free and lifting the hatch. A blast of cold air rushes out, along with the smell of *vinarhi*. Violets. The scent's so strong it makes my stomach turn.

Daniel stares at him. 'I thought you didn't use technology?'

I raise my eyebrows. Daniel's right, the padlock is from Earth.

'The Ether is unpredictable this far into the bedrock,' Illortha says. 'The boundaries are thin and erratic. The rock-crystal we use for building doesn't take root this far down.'

'The cell has been here for a thousand years,' Rashae says. Her expression tells me this is another mystery she doesn't have an explanation for. 'And it serves its purpose. There is no escape from this place, not even for those who are skilled in working the Ether.'

Below the hatch is a spiral staircase. It's narrow enough that we have to walk in single file. Thick, white cloud curls up around me in wisps of vapour. I can hardly see anything except for a few of those globe lights in the distance. It's hard to see where I'm putting my feet, and once we reach a solid floor I realise we're not standing in a room but on an island in the centre of a huge cavern. It's bigger than a soccer field. I can't see the walls and even the jagged ceiling is so high in most places that it's invisible.

'Wow,' Daniel breathes.

Vinarhi spreads around the island in a swirling, rushing torrent. The sound fills my ears and echoes through the cavern.

There are other islands. I can see them as grey silhouettes behind the veil of *vinarhi* mist.

Thin ridges of rock-crystal poke above the surface of the mist, making bridges and walkways between the islands that cross the swirling lightness of the water like gossamer webs.

It's not what I imagined.

'This is the prison?' I say.

Pain suddenly twinges in my ankle and I give a yelp of pain.

'The charm is wearing off,' Illortha says kindly. 'You'll have limited mobility from now on but do not strain yourself. As your leg heals, you'll be able to move normally.'

'Normally?' I say. 'As in, completely healed?'

'I can't say for certain. I don't know how well you will heal. But yes, you will notice an improvement.'

I hold onto those words so tightly. I'm so glad to hear him say them that I almost run across to hug him. Then a sudden thought seizes my heart, crushing it in my chest.

'You're still going to kill us, aren't you?'

They head for the stairway without answering.

'Hey!' I yell. 'Hey! How much longer have I got? Why did you bother curing me if you're just going to kill me?' There's no reply.

'Fuck you!' I spit at them. 'I hate you!'

The only answer is the sound of the hatch lowering back into place, then the sharp click of the lock.

I look at Daniel. His face is pale. 'They're going to kill us?'

'Oh,' I say, kicking myself. Stupid, stupid, *stupid!* 'Well, no. Not really.'

'Not really? What does that mean?'

'It's . . . it's hard to explain.' I can't think of anything else to tell him. He'll know if I'm lying and I don't want to lie to him, anyway. 'But, well, yes. I guess they think we're too much of a threat to leave lying around.'

I look around our new home, wondering if I can try to balance across one of the rock ridges and see where it leads, but despair has dropped a thick, heavy blanket over me. I drop to sit on one of the jagged rocks, it's as cold as metal, and put my head in my hands. How long will they give us before they do it. A week? A month? A day? Once I'm part of the Ether, will I be able to come back and haunt them?

All that time I spent thinking about death in the Sanatorium, and whether I'd like to choose my own time and place to die. It seems like waste of effort now that I'll be killed regardless of what I want.

'I don't want to die,' Daniel says.

I don't want to die either. It's crazy to even think about it.

I've got a whole life I want to live. There are all these things I always thought I'd do and now, I can't believe I'm not going to be able to do them.

'We're not going to die.' I say, hoping that by saying it out loud, I'll believe it too.

'They won't sentence you to *valatha*.'

It's a female voice, soft and gentle and somehow familiar although I can't see the speaker through the haze.

'What?' I say, then realise that's not what I want to ask. 'I mean, why not? Who are you?'

I squint into the misty light, and I just can make her out. She balances lightly across one of the ridges; a slender girl with the typical Sharian pale blond hair.

I hear Daniel gasp and, before I can hold him back, he rushes towards her.

'You're here!' he says, sliding to a stop and looking as if he wants to hug her but won't. 'You're here!' he repeats.

'Keira?' It's another voice, but one I recognise instantly. It's so welcoming that I wonder if my imagination has conjured it.

'Archon?'

He answers, proving he's more than just a hallucination. Stepping around the girl, he comes towards me with a smile on his face, a real smile, one he must have inherited from his father. A smile that sparkles in his too-colourful eyes.

'I didn't think I'd ever see you again,' he says. He stops short of actually touching me, and I'm left wishing he would.

'Well, it's not like we can actually *see* anything much down here,' I quip. 'But yeah, I thought the same. I guess it's a good thing you have so few options when it comes to places for locking people up in this city.'

'And I didn't think I would see either of you again,' says the girl. She looks between us, her eyes shining. See us *again*? *Who is she?* 'What I told you is true,' she continues. 'They won't sentence you to *valatha*. It's only a ruse to appease the public and to hide their real intentions.'

'Oh,' I say. 'What are their real intentions?'

It's Archon who replies. 'They want to study you. Find out everything they can.'

'Oh, you mean like *you* wanted to,' I remind him, and in the dim, misty light I can see he's blushing. I give a relenting sigh. 'It's okay. I'm getting used to being a museum piece.'

'Don't be fooled,' the girl says, and again I think how familiar her voice is. But the mist keeps wreathing around her face, sending rainbows sparkling in her hair, so I can't see her properly. I can barely see her lips move as she speaks. 'Chief Arbitrator Iranth won't harm you because you're too valuable to her and her plans. But the "experience" won't be pleasant. Humans are fragile and experience pain more easily than our people.'

I can hear a thousand thoughts whirling between us.

'I'm just sorry that this happened to you,' she continues. 'When Archon told me you were both here, I was so worried. I only wish I could have helped.'

'You know, you people really should work on your optimism. We're not dead. We're not hurt.

I'm not going to give up looking for a way home.' I say this, then wonder if I really believe it. I shake my head, still staring at her, trying to place that half-glimpsed face and soft voice. 'Who *are* you?'

'My name is Cari,' she says. 'And it's my fault you're here.'

Chapter 23
Between the Worlds

I GAPE. Yeah, my mouth is actually hanging open. Had she been here, Mum would've warned me about swallowing flies.

'What do you mean?' I choke out at last.

'*I* am here because I was sentenced to three years imprisonment for breaking the Edict. I did so in the worst way possible . . . I punched a hole in the fabric of the boundary and, because of this, I let part of my world into yours.'

'I endangered not only my world but yours as well. It was a terrible mistake. I am so sorry, Keira.'

I recognise her voice, now. I should have recognised it from the start. But she's changed. She's thinner, smaller and her ice-blue eyes are haunted. No wonder my own eyes reminded me of someone else in the mirror. They looked like *hers*. But it's incredible, unbelievable –

'Rebecca?'

I *can* see her now. She emerges from the mist, the sparkling light of the *vinarhi* clinging to her like dewdrops. The crystal shard is working its magic and suddenly I can see her aura, the faint blue-green tinge of gentle curiosity that I could only associate with one person. The girl who Jake fell in love with.

This is who I saw when I looked at myself in the ice at Sarinne's house, when I had the shard inside me. The ice-angel.

And then it finally hits me. She's the one who created the blizzard, who brought the ice and the snow from Shar. I shake my head, still not quite able to wrap my mind around the fact that this girl, the one I was talking to only a week ago *on my* world, when everything was normal, is not human. Unfortunately it makes too much sense. The only girl good enough for Jake Miles is one from another world.

'Please tell me,' she says, and I can tell she's been dying to ask this since I arrived. 'About Jake.'

'He's okay,' Daniel says. 'We got stuck in the snowstorm and I hurt my knee, but we got home okay. Nina yelled at us, though.'

I interject, remembering that night. The snowstorm and thinking I was going to die. 'I guess that's what you all get for trying to rescue me. Now we're stuck here and –'

I don't intend it to sound bitter, but it does. I don't blame her for me being here, not exactly. But if she hadn't been fooling around with things she didn't understand, I never would have gone through this whole ankle thing at all!

'I didn't mean for any of this to happen,' she says quietly. 'I only used the bridge because I wanted to learn more . . . to see more of your world. But when my mother discovered what I'd done. I . . . I ran. I might have died if Jake hadn't found me.'

I try to ignore the warmth in her voice when she mentions Jake. 'Well, you got through to my world, there's got to be a way for us to go back. How did you punch your way through in the first place? Can't we use it to get home?'

'What I did was difficult; it's not something you can just *do*. I always wanted to be a Healer. But when time came for my assignment, I was given to the Guild of Librarians. While I was in one of the libraries, I found a book. It told me all about Earth and, from that moment, I was amazed. I started to research the ways to cross between the worlds. I stole manuscripts that I wasn't supposed to read and found information I wasn't supposed to know. Eventually, I found a bridge.'

She smiles at this memory. 'This was one of the stable ones that still remained open. I traced its location to a secret place in the corner of a park. There is a way to unravel a string from a bridge and push it through the boundary, so that's what I did. It was hard work and it took me a long time, but I did it. And when I went to that park and held the string in my hands, I could listen to the reverberations along it.

But the workers in the Etherium discovered my disruption. They knew I'd found a bridge and that I'd been using it, though they didn't know exactly how. I overheard a member of their guild talking to my mother, telling her what I'd done. I knew she wouldn't take me to the Guardians but she couldn't stop them coming for me.' She stops talking for a moment, and her voice becomes softer. 'I was so scared. I ran to the bridge, thinking I could hide. But my mother found me. She knew exactly where I would go.

'She was angry with me, and when she cut the bridge from under me I thought it was because she was angry. But now … now I think she did it so that the Guardians couldn't find me and punish me for what I'd done … but it doesn't matter why. When she cut the bridge, I fell down into your world. But the Guardians didn't know about the thread I'd pushed through and that Earth was suffering because of it. I had to return, to tell them what I'd done, and fix it. So that's what I did. The Guardians healed the rift. Then they tried me for my crimes.'

She looks at me calmly, her aura pulsing with dark areas that I know are genuine sorrow.

'Do you think I would still be here if I could make a stable bridge? Believe me, I've tried!' She looks down at her feet, ashamed. 'But down here, every time I try to work with the Ether, it slips out of my grasp. There are bridges here, thousands of them. The fabric is so thin! But if you tried, you'd be torn apart in an instant. The Guardians are not stupid. They wouldn't use this place if they thought for a second anyone could escape.'

'That is the thing about the boundary. It *wants* to keep the balance. It wants to keep our worlds apart because it *has* to. But, sometimes, the balance shifts to accommodate a person who has crossed to keep itself in order, I think. There is the possibility that you're too changed by being in this world to return. There are people from my world who have crossed into yours and haven't been able to come back. I was warned . . .'

'But it must work the other way, too. Why aren't there any people from our world living here?'

'I wondered that myself. I spent time trying to find them, when I was a Novice.' Her voice is sad. 'There are humans in the city, but they are kept hidden. If they're allowed to live among us, the Edict would keep them from speaking out. Although the humans wouldn't do any- thing without provocation, the Guardians won't hesitate to sentence them to enforced *valatha* if they cause any problems.'

She sighs.

'Doesn't anyone ever find a way back?' I ask in a small voice.

'There are ways. Perhaps some of them have, over the years.'

Of course! Visitors to fairyland. People with stories of UFO abductions. The nutcases I've always laughed at. Maybe they had come here and were lucky enough to return.

Chapter 24
Finding a Way

THERE is no place here to sleep, Archon tells me. We make do on the flat ground. It's cold and uncomfortable but I've spent so much time lying down these past few days that if I never see another bed again, I'll be happy.

I walk across some of the ridges, exploring alone while Daniel talks enthusiastically with Cari/Rebecca and Archon sits quietly, occupied by his own thoughts. The smell of the *vinarhi* grows stronger, until it fills my nose, making my head ache. Some of the islands are steep and rocky, some are so flat they're barely above the surface of the *vinarhi*. There are a few plants; some scrubby trees, different from the trees above. They're not tall and crystalline but short and stumpy with broad flat leaves. Both kinds are pale, I notice, and, in some ways, a cross between the trees of my world and those of Shar.

I crouch down at the edge of the rock and watch the *vinarhi* tumbling by beneath my feet. I reach out a finger and feel the cool refreshing touch of it, but it's rougher than the stuff I bathed in at Sarinne's house. It almost stings.

I pick up one of the fallen leaves. Only it's not really a leaf, I realise, but a *pod*, like a huge half-gumnut about as wide as my arm.

I toss it into the rushing torrent and watch as it bobs along the surface, holding still for a moment, and whirling away when caught by the current. I keep watching until it disappears.

I make my way back, slipping once and wrenching my ankle so badly I have to sit there for twenty minutes gritting my teeth against the pain. It begins to fade, thankfully, but I vow to take it easy. Ten minutes after that, I'm restlessly roaming again.

It's even harder to tell how much time has passed down here.

At one point the hatch above us clanks open and several packages wrapped in cloth are dropped down the staircase. They contain jars of some kind of stew, a loaf of something stodgy and white, a container of something like camomile tea, and a bundle of crystal cutlery. I'm hungry enough to eat everything and be disappointed there isn't more when I'm done.

I sit looking at the utensils they've given us to eat with. They're small and metallic, like a dessert spoon with little prongs on the end.

'You know,' I say, 'if this was a prison break movie, we could jerry-rig a lock-pick out of our sporks.'

Daniel laughs. Archon looks puzzled.

'Didn't you ever play cops and robbers when you were kids? If you got put in the slammer, you'd have to pick your way out . . .' I give up. Of course they don't know what cops and robbers are. They probably didn't play games when they were kids, either.

Instead, I drag myself back up the staircase and rattle the bars experimentally.

'Locks are mechanical,' I explain, feeling like I'm teaching little kids how to tie their shoelaces. 'They're made in a cylinder, with little pins inside. When you push the pins back in the right order, it releases the mechanism and the lock opens. That's what a key does; pushes the pins back.'

'It doesn't make sense. Why make something so easy to disarm? A coded crystal can only be unlocked by one that's been grown alongside it because the resonances match. Sometimes, the crystals are trained to respond only to a certain person's aura.' Archon sounds unimpressed. I guess our technology does sound kind of clumsy when you think about it.

Daniel, however, has the answer. 'They said the Ether doesn't work so well down here.'

I nod. 'They did, so maybe those magical crystals won't work either. They would have to use more . . . primitive methods. And I wonder who it was that built these cells. Maybe our ancestors are closer than you think.'

'Impossible,' says Archon. 'Shar has existed for millennia. It is the First City and the Last.

Your world wasn't even born at the time these foundations were being hollowed out by the forces of nature.'

'Yeah, but we share a lot of things, don't we? Look at us. We all have arms, legs, heads and torsos, right? We don't have tentacles or, like, five noses or something. We're pretty similar in appearance. Doesn't that at least make you think we might have something in common? Like, maybe our ancestors were related in some way?'

There's no answer from either of them. I jam the end of my spork into the padlock and wriggle it. It's the wrong shape and I've never picked a lock in my life so I've got no idea what I'm doing, but I have to do *something*.

I hear footsteps coming along the corridor above, and I've just got time to hide the spork before I see who it is.

It's Arina, and her mother, Sarinne. They're led by the same young man who'd been at the desk earlier.

'Thank you, Delth,' says Sarinne. 'You are dismissed.'

He nods. 'Let me know if you have any difficulties,' he says.

Sarinne watches him depart, then turns to me. She kneels and, through the bars of the hatch, it looks as if she's putting on a brave face.

Apprehensively, Arina stops a few steps away.

'I'm here to monitor you,' Sarinne says. 'I'm supposed to report on your condition.'

'Well, I'll do my best to make an interesting report. Why did they send you, though? I would've thought they'd want to keep you away from your wicked son . . . and brother.' I add, for Arina's benefit.

'We've been sent here on official business, of course. Arina is here to check your healing progress, Keira. And I am required to monitor prisoners regularly.' Sarinne gives an ironic almost-smile. 'But oh, believe me, there's another purpose behind it. They want me to see Archon. They want Arina to see him. He's an example to us, you see; and to the rest of Shar. We are disgraced, and they want to show us how badly. They want us to tell others so that everyone will think twice about making the same mistakes.'

Once again, I'm impressed by the arrogance of the Guardians. They really think they can manipulate people so easily by trying to scare them. Can't they see how badly something like this might backfire? Didn't they ever think that Arina, instead of being intimidated by her brother's imprisonment, might resent the treatment and those who enforced it?

They're turning her against them. And Sarinne, I think, has already been turned. It's just a question of how far . . .

I smile to myself.

'Sarinne!' Archon calls out from below. He climbs the stairs, and peers over my shoulder. I don't need the shard's influence. I can feel how close he is by the tingling of my skin.

'Oh, Archon,' says Sarinne, and something seems to break through her resolve. She reaches through the bars and takes his hand. I can see the colours pulse between them. They're saying things with the *ihlwarh*, and I suddenly wish I wasn't standing here between them.

Suddenly Archon freezes. 'Arina, what's is that?'

'What?' she asks.

'Shh!' he hisses, and then I hear it too. It's a low humming sound, irregular, pulsing. It's . . . it's a dial tone!

Chapter 25
Cari and Jake

'ARINA?'

She reaches into her robes and pulls out my phone. The useless phone I gave to her. The sound is impossibly loud, pulled from the tinny little speakers by the gaps in reality, echoing down into the depths of the space below.

'What's it doing?' Arina asks, panic in her voice. 'Is it about to speak again?'

I reach through the bars. 'Give it to me. Please!'

She hesitates for a moment, and then comes close enough to put it in my hand. I take it gratefully, tap the screen, and find it lights up with the words "call connected". I check the number. Jake's contact photo smiles back at me.

The phone clicks, and for a moment, I just stare at it. I can *see* it. A shimmering golden thread spins out from the phone and plunges down into the chamber below before vanishing into the *vinarhi*.

Then a faint, crackling sound comes through the speakers.

'Jake?' I say tentatively.

'Keira!'

It echoes: *Keira . . . ra . . . ra . . .*

'Jake! Jake, it's me!' I'm shouting, putting the phone close to my mouth, wanting to be sure he can hear me. 'Jake, I'm stuck. I stole your telescope and I . . . Daniel is . . .'

'Keira, Keira, shhh!' he says. 'Shut up and listen. I know, okay? I know. I'm so glad you and Daniel are okay. I've been . . . shit . . . I've been so worried. I ran to your house but, by the time I got there, you were gone and so was Daniel. I didn't know what to do . . . and then I spoke to that girl, Arina, who said you were both okay, but it's been *hours . . .*'

'Hours?' Daniel says. 'But we've been here for days, Jake!'

'Time runs differently in Shar,' Cari explains over his shoulder. 'An hour might pass on Earth, while a day could pass here.'

'Jake, it's amazing,' I break-in. 'They cured my leg . . . I think they did but –'

But I'm *not* okay, really, am I?

'We're in a jail, Jake. They don't exactly like humans here. They're only keeping us alive so they can learn more about Earth. Jake . . . they want to destroy us, I think. All of humanity. All of Earth.'

'What –'

'Cari says –'

'Cari?'

Cari . . . ri . . . ri . . .

There is a moment, then, a moment that you can *feel*. I can see it, like the auras. It's so real it's palpable. It's Cari and Jake. It's their connection coming across the distance in waves, swirling through the room, filling even the abyss below.

I've heard the term "soul mates". I have to muffle my snorts of laughter when Mum says she felt that way about Dad. I mean, he decided he'd rather live in London than with her and his daughter, so I kind of have a cynical view when it comes to *fate*, *destiny* and all that.

But if there is such a thing as a mystical cosmic connection between two people, this is it.

I'm jealous but I like to think I'm handling it well.

'Jake,' Cari says. Although her voice isn't that loud, I know he'll hear her. We're not talking via the phone anymore. I think we needed the phone to make the connection but, now that it's punched a hole in the boundary, it's working like a signal tower and relaying our voices.

'Jake,' she repeats. 'I'm so glad to hear your voice. I was beginning to think that you weren't real. That I imagined it all . . .'

'Me, too,' Jake's voice is quiet and full of something I've only ever heard once before; when he was talking to me, that moment before we almost kissed. 'It seems like it happened a million years ago. I didn't think I'd ever hear from you again.'

'We are part of the balance. I think there is more to happen between us.'

It's a conversation no one else should be listening to. I grit my teeth and try not to think about punching Cari in her picture-perfect-face when Sarinne interrupts from above.

'Arina and I will be expected to return soon,' she says. 'We cannot waste any time.'

I'm relieved it wasn't me who disrupted the moment between Jake and Cari. 'We need to figure out how to escape. We have to get back. If we stay here . . . ' I shiver, thinking of what they'll do to me, Daniel and Cari, even Archon, to find out about Earth.

'You have the telescope,' says Jake. 'Mrs . . . someone I know used it to find a bridge to cross into our world, Keira.'

'Yes,' I say slowly. 'But Jake, any bridge would be torn apart down here.'

Cari breaks in, her voice low and urgent. 'Keira!' She points to the golden thread still running from the phone our heads. 'I told you the Ether is unpredictable down here, that I can't create a bridge with no foundation. What you call the *magic* of our world won't work. But what about the magic of yours?'

I think I know what she's talking about. 'Technology? But we don't have anything to work with.'

'All we need is something to hold us while we navigate the currents. We have the thread of the phone to guide us. If we can use this telescope, we can follow it through the boundary and back into your world!'

My heart flutters for a moment but my excitement is quickly swallowed by despair. I hang my head. *Damn it!* 'I don't have it. I lost the telescope when I came through.'

No one says anything.

'I'm sorry, Jake.' I babble. 'I know Mrs Henders gave it to you. I met a man who knew her. He told me everything. And I've gone and lost it . . . I can't believe I was so stupid . . .'

'Keira,' says Sarinne, her voice low and urgent as she reaches into her robes. 'I have a confession to make.'

'What?'

'I found your . . . telescope. Soon after you arrived, I noticed it in the garden, and I hid it. I recognised it for what it was; a Forbidden Object. I intended to give it to the Guardians, but I hesitated. It was a connection, you see, with your world. The same world that my . . . that Archon's father came from. I wanted to keep it.'

Chapter 26
It's Not Yours

I'M ANGRY. Oh yes, I'm angry. I don't think I've ever been so angry in my life. It's like a beating drum inside my chest. 'What? You selfish –' I remind myself that she's an adult and I'm supposed to show respect, but what she's done is unforgivable. 'You could have sent us home days ago!'

She removes her hand and in it is a dark blue cloth. Folding it back she reveals the telescope.

'WHAT? You have it with you?' I'm aghast, and surprised. Rashae had said they run the security crystals over everyone who comes down here. 'How . . . why didn't the Guardians take it off you when you came down here?'

'They would have, if the scanning crystal had been able to see it. However . . .'

I laugh out loud. 'That's Archon's magical cloth, isn't it? The one he hid his dad's watch in. I saw it . . .' I look over my shoulder at him. 'You shared it with me during the *ihlwarh*, when I saw your memories.'

He answers slowly, staring at his mother with wide eyes. 'Yes. I did the best I could to keep that watch from them, but they discovered my deception. I had to turn it over to them. But they didn't know about the cloth. I kept that for myself.'

I stare at the telescope. It's a shining beacon. My only hope.

'Give it to me,' I say.

But Archon steps in front of me, his eyes glistening. 'This belongs here,' he says. 'It belongs in this world. Sarinne, you need to take it to the Etherium! You need to get them to study it and figure out how it works.'

'No,' Jake's voice comes through the phone. 'It's mine. The person who made it gave it to *me*. Keira, you have to bring it back!'

I glare at Archon. 'You can't keep it. It's not yours.' I try not to look at Daniel, knowing that he used the same words with me a short time ago.

'It's not yours either!' Archon protests desperately. 'I've looked for this . . . for something like this . . . for so long. This is the object that could change our world forever. With something like this, people will believe in the changes that we need. I can confront the Council. Mother, we can't just let it go.'

'You have to!' I almost shout. 'This is our way home!'

He steps forwards, closer to me. He looks into my eyes. 'You don't have to leave, Keira.'

I push him away, putting all of my anger into it. He feels the physical force and the jolt of anger through the *ihlwarh*. He stumbles and falls back against the rail.

'Why, so we can stay here and give you more information about my world?!' I yell. 'You want me to give up my life so you can learn about computers and dogs and . . . what else? Guns? Bombs? What do you really want? Knowledge that you can keep to yourself so you've got an edge over the Guardians? Or over the Below World?'

He's bleeding. There's a gash on his lip, and I'm shocked to see dark red blood oozing out of it. He pulls himself to his feet and takes a step down the stairs. He's unsteady on his feet, swaying a bit.

'No,' he says quietly. 'You're wrong. I don't want you to leave, Keira. But not because I want to know more about your world, although I do, desperately. It's because I like you, Keira. I like being in your presence.'

His words are so unexpected, so astonishing, that I literally gulp. My heart skips a beat. Even without using the crystal, I can see he means every word he says, and it *scares* me. No one's ever said anything like this to me.

'I didn't realise . . .' I don't know how to end that sentence. The gash on his forehead is trickling blood. Without knowing what I'm doing, I reach out to wipe it with my finger. It's red and sticky and slightly warm.

'We have the same blood,' I say slowly.

I pull myself away from him. I feel awkward because I've just realised that everyone is looking at us, including his mother.

Fumbling with my hands, I look at Sarinne. She's standing so close. Her eyes are moving between me and her son. There's a war going on inside her.

'I risked so much to bring this here,' she says. 'If I give you the telescope, they'll know someone helped you escape. They'll know it was me,' she says.

'Yes,' I say slowly.

But then Cari speaks. 'But you know it's the right thing to do. Keira has to go home.'

'How can you know that it's the right thing?' Archon says.

'She was badly injured and was sent here because she needed to be cured. I have a feeling that now this has been done, she is meant to go home. Why else would she be here, along with us, and the telescope, and the phone? In one place, at the same time? Can't you see that?'

Everyone goes quiet. The rushing of the *vinarhi* echoes in my ears.

'We can't wait any longer,' she says. 'If the connection the phone has made with your world breaks, we may never get it back.'

She looks back at Sarinne. 'Look at the influence she's had already. The people she's touched. And think of what will happen if the Guardians begin to work on her.'

'They'll do what they did to my husband,' she says quietly. 'They'll take her life by force. And the boy's, as well.'

'Worse than that. They'll destroy the world your husband came from. He might be gone, but his family, his relations . . . Archon's family . . . they still live there. Are you willing to do that?'

There is a pause and Sarinne steps closer to the bars. 'I ask you one thing in return,' she says, as she passes telescope to Cari, 'I took this risk for one reason, and one reason only. I needed to know that my son was safe. Keira, you must take Archon with you.'

'What?' he breathes out and I feel it against my ear. 'Sarinne, I –'

'You must go, Archon. You're not safe here. If you stay, they'll enforce *valatha* –'

'I don't want to leave!' he sounds panicked. 'Not without you and Arina. How can I –'

He shoves past me and rattles the hatch desperately. It doesn't give an inch.

Sarinne reaches through the bars once more, takes his hand and I see the ebb and flow of their auras as they share *ihlwarh*. 'This is the right thing, Archon. Just as the girl said.'

'I never . . . I never belonged here, did I?' he says miserably.

'The balance, the Ether, called to you. Through all these years, you've been chasing your father's world. And if the balance ever calls you back, you will be able to share everything you've learned with us. This is very important, Archon.'

'Are you sure?'

'How can any of us be sure?' she smiles slightly. 'But it feels right, doesn't it?'

He gives a slow nod. 'Yes, it does.'

Sarinne turns away. 'We have to go.'

Arina looks at her brother, her face carefully expressionless but, in her eyes, I can see a tempest of emotion. 'I will . . . I will miss you,' she says. Then she whirls around and runs back up the passageway.

Sarinne glances over her shoulder as she reluctantly follows.

We're left alone at last, the four of us: a girl who breaks the barriers of the worlds, a kid who's able to believe in the impossible, a boy who doesn't know which one he belongs to and me, who is starting to think I don't know, either. How, in a thousand universes, did we all come together?

Chapter 27
Keira versus the Guardians

WE GROUP at the bottom of the staircase, close to the edge of the island.

'Are you still there, Jake?' I ask.

'Yes. What are you doing?'

'I really have no idea,' I let out a stupid giggle, feeling nervous, scared and hopeful all at the same time. 'Remember the treehouse?'

Jake laughs too. 'Of course. We spent ages making that.'

The others look puzzled, even Daniel doesn't know what I intend to do. I'm glad I've got something only I can share with Jake. This is one thing Cari won't understand.

'Okay,' I say, pointing at the scrubby little trees. 'We need some of these. Tear the branches off. Get the straightest ones if you can, and keep them as long as possible.'

They look at me as if I'm crazy.

'Trust me, it'll make sense soon.'

I'm enjoying being in charge. This is what I'm supposed to be, doing things, making stuff happen. It feels good to be in control after all these weeks of having things decided for me; first my operation, being forced across the bridge, the Guardians, the healing of my ankle, then this horrible imprisonment.

Both Cari and Archon seem hesitant about breaking the trees. I have to stop my own work to watch them. I don't think I've seen either of them do something so physical.

'This is wrong,' says Cari, her hands gripping the branch. 'This tree is a living thing. This will hurt it.'

'Hurt it?' I laugh, then I realise she's serious. 'But it's just a tree.'

'It lives and grows,' she says softly.

'Well, if you want to stay here, go ahead,' I say, suddenly annoyed.

She closes her eyes and pushes down the branch. There's a loud crack and for a moment I feel a sickening lurch in my stomach. I glance at Cari and realise she's felt it too; that this is what she was talking about. I wonder if it's the crystal shard, or whether it's just how much I've changed by being here.

'We don't have a choice,' I whisper to Cari, to the tree, to myself.

We get about two dozen of the branches and a couple of the huge pods. Daniel piles them neatly and I sit down with my spork and saw the extra twigs and leaves off them. I untie the sash from around my waist. The shard falls free, and I place it carefully to one side. I wind the sash through the branches, but it isn't long enough.

'I'll need yours, as well.'

The others take their sashes off. Daniel's is plain, like mine. Cari's, I see, is black, and I suddenly recall one similarity between some cultures on Earth and that of Shar; black is used to symbolise death.

Archon is reluctant to hand his over. I know how much it means to him; he loves his life task more than anything and now, well . . . he'll probably never get the First Level Access he wants so much.

Daniel holds back as well.

'What?' I demand.

'Are you going to tie it all together like you and Jake did the floorboards for the treehouse?'

'Yeah.'

'It's just . . . I remember it fell apart, like, ten times.'

I glare at him. 'That's an exaggeration.'

'Can I help?'

'No.' I say, a little too sharply. I don't want any interruptions. He ducks his head and hands me his sash. I try to recall exactly how I did it. It's been a few years, but as I weave the makeshift rope through the branches, knotting it as I go, it starts to come back to me. I try not to think about Daniel's words. There's not going to be any room for mistakes here.

As I work, I hold the shard in one hand and I can feel my fingers start to tingle. It feels like when I pushed through the restraint that first time in Sarinne's house, drawing bits and pieces together, making them into one solid thing. I breathe deeply and pour the strength I feel into what my hands are doing.

I look up when I've finished to find Daniel looking crestfallen. I feel bad for snapping at him.

'Here,' I tell him. 'Hold this.' I give him the shard to look after. He eyes it suspiciously but takes it. I don't want to let it go but I need both my hands free now.

What I have is a platform about the size of Mum's kitchen table. With the loose ends of the sashes, I tie some of the large gumnut pods around the bottom edge. It kind of looks like a boat and it's the best we're going to get.

Archon and I lift it over the edge of the island. It slides into the *vinarhi* and bobs slightly, then the current takes over and tries to pull it out of our hands, but there's no way I'm letting go.

There are gaps in it. The buffeting current is going to whip it around easily. But it's floating.

It's strong. I *wove* it. It'll hold together.

I'm pretty proud of myself.

I pick up the telescope. It's warm and, while I can't be sure, it seems to be *quivering*; shaking like Molly does when she's all fired up for a walk and waiting for the door to open.

I squint through the lens. I can still see the islands and the *vinarhi*, the blank greyness in the distance. And I can see other things, too. It's like lightning, if you could slow it down enough to see how it rips through the air. Through the gaps I can see ... other things. Buildings, I think, in one place. Tall skyscrapers. In another, something moves. It's a big, black-furred animal, like a huge panther, peering at me with green eyes. Another rip floats in front of it, and there's a sunshine-filled field, a woman brushing her hair in the next, an ocean with bright yellow water, a chimney belching smoke ...

'How many worlds are there?' I ask, handing the telescope to Archon and taking the phone, with its golden thread stretching and wavering. I step up to the edge of the *vinarhi*.

Cari answers. 'Nobody can be certain. Thousands upon thousands, perhaps.'

'Really?' Daniel asks, awed. 'Do you think there's one with dinosaurs?'

'Our two worlds are closest,' adds Archon. 'Earth and Shar. It's been a topic of debate since time began as to why.'

I look out at the violent flow and wonder ... if any of us loses our grip, there's no telling where we'll end up.

I look back at the others. I know we don't have a choice.

Taking a deep breath, I step onto the raft. It rocks under me and even though I'm expecting it and I'm crouching low, I almost lose my balance and go sliding over the edge. I clutch the phone tightly with one hand, the golden beam still visible through the *vinarhi*.

'Come on,' I say to Daniel. He steels himself and, with a look of determination, steps onto the raft. It rocks as he sits down, then settles as he stops moving.

'Here,' I say, giving him the phone and reclaiming the shard. It settles into my hand comfortably.

There's a shout from above us. It echoes loudly down the staircase.

'It's them,' Daniel says, making the raft rock again as he tries to stand and see up the staircase.

I have a feeling they're pretty mad.

I can see Archon's aura. He's brown-grey; scared. I grab him by the sleeve.

'Step away from the edge!' commands Guardian Rashae. She's using the Ether now, or trying to. Her hands work the air madly, but nothing is happening. 'Stop what you're doing immediately! Overseer Delth! The key, quickly!'

But Delth fumbles and drops the key. He's not used to using such clumsy tools, I guess. He lunges after it and Rashae, hissing in anger, snatches it up herself.

'Every one of you,' another voice rings out, and I recognise the icy-cold tone belonging to Chief Arbitrator Iranth, 'is in violation of the Edict. Stay where you are and you won't be harmed.'

It's not an empty threat. She's working the Ether herself, using her hands to pluck at the air in front of her. A sudden wind whips me in the face, stealing my breath and, in a moment, I realise what she's doing. She's not trying to create anything new. She's picking up the wild currents of the fractured Ether and throwing it at us.

It's a good tactic. In seconds, all I can see is whirling grey mist. The others vanish and the raft rocks dangerously.

'Keira!' I hear Cari's voice. Where is she? My hair whips into my face. I take a deep breath and it's full of cold, violet-scented mist.

'Cari, take my hand,' I reach out to where she should be. I can just see her colours, the calm blue that I only associate with her. I yank her forwards, almost off her feet. She yelps and nearly falls on top of me but I'm ready for it and use her momentum to pull her onto the raft. It bobs and splashes, drenching us both. 'Daniel, can you help her?'

Daniel takes her hand, and the colour red pulses between them. Cari winds her fingers through one of the sashes and the raft steadies.

But where's Archon? I can't feel him anymore.

'Stay here and hold the raft,' I bark at Daniel, jumping back onto the island. It's much worse now, like standing in the middle of a tornado.

I squeeze the shard, feeling the sharp edges dig into my palm. I need to concentrate, but it's so hard with the wind whipping and the noise in my ears . . .

Focus, I have to focus.

When you're out on the soccer field, you have to tune out the sounds of the crowd. Pretend they're not even there, especially during the bigger games, when everyone's yelling, cheering and, importantly, *watching* every move you make. Because if you take a single moment to look at two mothers clobbering each other with hotdogs, you can miss the perfect kick. It's one of the first things you learn, and something Mr Alderston drills into us constantly. Focus on the game.

The more I think about it, the more this whole thing feels like a soccer game. The field is a bit different; but there's a goal, the bridge, which I have to reach; and players, me and Archon, who I have to keep track of.

And then the others step onto the field. The Guardians are shadows; tall, distorted figures looming up ahead of us. Rashae, Illortha and Chief Arbitrator Iranth are the opposing team blocking the way to victory.

'Archon!' I scream. I can see him, or at least, I can see his aura; the greyish yellow of indecision. I can tell he wants to obey the Guardians, not me.

I see him standing there, unable to move, the telescope hanging loosely in his hands.

I can feel the adrenaline, along with a horrible pulling sensation as the Ether tries to tear me to pieces. But there's no way I'm throwing away this game. I pretend there's a talent scout on the sidelines, and I'm going to impress him so badly he won't be able to resist offering me a place on the state team . . .

I dodge to the left, then right. My ankle protests, but I ignore it. The pain isn't unbearable, nothing compared to what I've been through the past few weeks. I reach out and grab Archon by the shoulder, feeling the shock of the *ihlwarh* as I show him my happiest memories of home.

My Mum, with her tired smile but happy eyes . . . The smell of bread as she brings home leftovers from work . . . I let him feel the comforting weight of Molly curled up at the end of my bed and the warm glow of pride I feel when Mr Alderston congratulates me on a goal . . .

All the things I miss.

But then all the other stuff leaks in, too. Like how much I've come to like him as a person.

'I like you, Keira. I like being in your presence.'

I show him how surprised I was that he would say that and mean it. I let him know that those words will stay in my memory forever and how scared I am that if he stays here, he'll be hurt . . .

'Archon,' I say. 'We have to go. Now.'

'Stay where you are!' commands Iranth. She reaches out and a sudden gust knocks into us. Archon stumbles. The telescope is ripped out of his hands. It pinwheels, end over end, tumbling into the *vinarhi* and vanishing from sight.

'No!' I yell. My horror is echoed by the Guardians and Archon, who suddenly breaks out of his sleep-like trance.

This is the shock he needed to pull him out of the Guardian's thrall, I've reached him. He backs away from the Guardians. Iranth has stepped down onto the island, her pale face alive with anger, but she's too slow. I shove Archon towards where the raft should be. Naturally more graceful than me, he leaps aboard. I feel like a clumsy idiot as I follow him, awkwardly stumbling onto raft and I push us away from the edge. I slip my wrist under one of the knots and hold on.

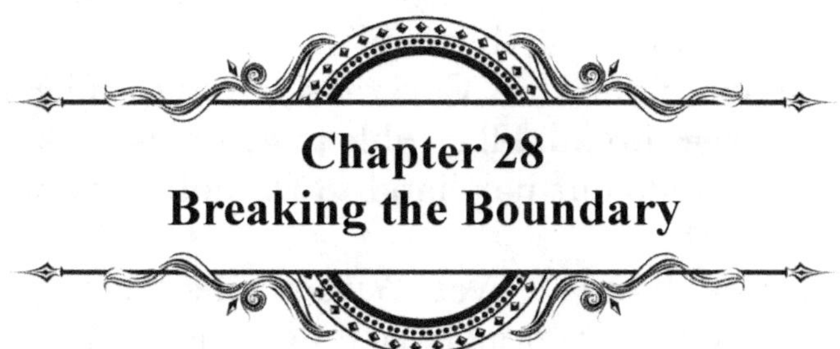

Chapter 28
Breaking the Boundary

THE raft rocks wildly as it encounters the raging currents. I've been on a boat exactly once in my life. That was on the lake just outside Cassidy Heights with my uncle, who decided I needed to learn how to fish. He'd picked a steaming hot day where there wasn't even a hint of a breeze. It was literally the most boring three hours of my life.

This time is completely different. The raft spins as the cross-currents try to take hold, lurching up and over unseen obstacles, bucking and tipping in the *vinarhi* as it tries to throw us off. The branches strain against my lashings and grind against one another. One of the pods comes free and is sucked under the *vinarhi*. I grit my teeth, not liking that I'm trusting my life to this.

But the best thing, the absolute best thing, is watching the silhouettes of the Guardians standing helplessly on the receding shore and knowing that the *vinarhi* has taken the telescope, and they'll never have it.

But neither will we.

'I lost it,' I say. 'I lost the telescope again. After all we went through!'

'It doesn't matter,' Cari reassures me, 'If I can follow the thread, I'll be able to guide us back.'

She holds out her hand to Daniel. 'Give me the phone.'

Daniel hands it over. Without the telescope, I can tell this is going to be tough and what will happen if she gets it wrong?

She closes her eyes. 'I can see it,' she says. 'Yes, I can see the fractures between the worlds! I can . . . if I . . .'

She lets go of the raft, balancing somehow without going overboard, and uses her free hand to work the air, plucking and twisting. The thread stretching from the phone starts to wind around itself. It glows brighter, looking more like a rope. The raft shivers as Cari fights the flow. Somehow, she manages to keep us on a steady course. Perspiration beads on her forehead. She's breathing hard.

'Cari? Keira? What's happening?' Jake pleads. I can barely hear him over the wind.

'She's pulling us through,' Daniel yells.

'It's amazing!' I call out. 'Jake, I wish you could see –'

'Ahh!' Cari gasps. Her hands are still moving. The golden thread is growing stronger. But her face . . . she's in pain.

'Cari?' I reach out to touch her shoulder but stop myself in time. If I touch her, the *ihlwarh* might disrupt what she's doing. 'Cari, are you okay?'

'It's . . . it's . . . I'm being . . . pressed between,' she gasps. 'It's too strong! . . . It . . . wants me. I could . . . slip . . . into it.'

Forget caution. I reach out and grab Cari's shoulder. The *ihlwarh* works instantly and I feel what she's feeling.

I see the *vinarhi* now. Not as I had before, a rushing river, but as Archon described it the first time he told me about it – as the *source*. It's a powerful force of constantly moving currents. Like an ocean in a storm, but . . . but it's *ordered*, every tiny part of it working with every other bit, together.

Cari's crouching in the middle of the currents and, as I'm pulled in with her, I shudder. It's like being in a wind tunnel. I can feel it tearing at my hair and clothes, whipping my skin, ripping my breath from me.

The thread. I can see the thread more clearly now than ever, stretching out in front of the raft. She's weaving it with her fingertips, it's rough in places, thin and almost transparent in others. The currents of the *vinarhi* are making it sway, threatening to shred it.

I scream into the noise. 'It's too dangerous.' I say. 'Leave it! We'll steer –'

'I can't! If I pull back now –'

I know what she means. Her colours, her aura, is being pulled by the currents. She's only holding herself back with the braided golden thread . . . and me.

I wrap my arms around her shoulders. With all my strength I yank backwards. Not just physically, but *mentally* as well, using the skill the crystal shard has given me to try and pull her back into herself. For a second, it works. Then I see the tendrils of my own aura being tugged into the currents.

'No!' I yell. I can feel it. Inside my chest, I can feel pieces of me being stretched and shredded.

Cari's hands are working frantically. 'I'm almost –'

'Keira! Keira!'

It's Archon's voice, but I can't see him. I can't see anything apart from Cari, the golden threads and the rippling colours of our auras.

I scream at her. 'Cari! You'll lose yourself! Leave it!'

'No!' She turns back to me, her eyes wide but her voice steady. 'No, I can get us through. I can do this.'

And then . . . and then she *does*.

I tumble back into myself. I'm gasping, amazed. I can see through the mist. There, below us, is a tree-lined street.

It's night-time, and the road glistens with rain. Streetlights shine on the puddles. A car races past, headlights glaring, showing a green wire fence with a letterbox shaped like a paddle-steamer, a ragged nature-strip and a discarded coke can. It's my world!

The raft shudders under us.

I'm not sure if I grabbed Archon, or he grabbed me, but somehow, his arms are wrapped around my shoulders. I can feel the *vinarhi* trying to tear us apart. Light streams out. I can feel the heat of it charring my skin and smell the smoke as my clothes start to smoulder. The thread pulls us onwards, rushing us towards the ground.

'Daniel!' I yell. *Where is he?*

'Keira!' It's Daniel, I can see him, clutching Archon's hand for dear life. 'Get Cari. Don't let her go!'

'I'm not going to!' I reach out for Cari.

'Keira!' she yells. Her voice is faint, like she's shouting over a huge distance. 'Keira, the thread, it's going to pull –'

I realise what she's trying to tell me. The golden thread that's guiding us is letting the silver light through into my world, the same way her thread breached the boundaries.

'Take my hand!' I yell.

She can't hear me. What's happening to her? I can't see . . . the glare of silver light behind her is too bright. All I can make out is the single golden wire from the phone she's still holding tightly.

'Cari! Cari!' I scream, and I hear Jake yelling it too, over and over again. But it's too late.

I squint and I can just make her out, but there's something separating us. Her eyes lock on mine, her lips move and though I can't hear what she says, I know what I have to do.

I have to cut the thread. It's strong and made out of the Ether, that strange substance I still don't understand. I know I can't tear it or break it; it's not of our world. There's only one thing that can cut it.

I reach into my sleeve and pull out the crystal shard. It looks more like a knife than ever. I don't want to do this.

I don't want to leave her there but . . . I don't have a choice.

I hesitate, looking at Cari. She nods.

I slash downwards. The thread breaks instantly, springing back like a taut wire. One end hits my wrist and vanishes. The other curls away into the distance.

With a crash, I hit the ground. Grass. It's wet, steaming and smoking. There are small patches of flames burning around us. My hand is wrenched backwards and my ankle screams, but I hardly feel it. I roll over and grab Archon's shoulder.

'Are you alright? Is everyone alright?' I stammer.

He's speechless for a moment, looking completely bewildered, but he shakes me off and sits up so I guess he's okay.

'Daniel?'

Daniel is lying a metre away. He rolls to his feet and looks upwards, but there's nothing to see except the night sky.

'Keira!' The shout is ringing, loud in the sudden silence. Someone is touching me, helping me sit up. I blink and see that it's Jake.

Jake!

We're on the front lawn of Jake's house, I realise. The link created by the phones must have pulled us through to where he, Daniel and Cari built a snowman a couple of weeks ago.

'Shit,' Jake says. 'You really did it.'

I want to run up and hug him. Before all this happened, I would have done exactly that without thinking twice. But now I'm thinking about our almost-kiss and how maybe it was only ever going to be an *almost*. I don't even want it to happen.

The house is dark behind him. Everyone's asleep except for us.

A few drops of rain fall, sizzling on the slowly dying embers around us.

Then Jake says: 'Where's Cari?'

And I start to cry.

Chapter 29
The Other World

THERE are hands on my shoulders, firm, steady hands, and. I look up into Mrs Henders wrinkled face.

When did she get here?

Everything seems to be happening to someone else. I watch from a distance as Daniel, Jake, Archon and I are led across to Mrs Henders' house. Inside, it's warm and comfortable. I sink onto a worn-in couch. A mug of something hot is passed to me. Tea with milk. I sip it gratefully. It tastes like how tea should taste.

I look up at the old woman who I've always thought of as a witch. Now that I know who she is, I can see the city in her. She is Sharian, but partly human as well. She's been changed.

Jake is speaking in a fast, panicked voice. 'We have to find her. We can't just leave her there.'

'You didn't see what happened to her!' Archon says. 'You didn't see where she was when we lost her. There's no way to get back there. No way to reach her.'

'We have to try! Mrs Henders —'

'Quiet,' barks the old woman, slamming her own cup of tea on the coffee table. 'This will get us nowhere. Calm yourself.'

'But she's —'

'You can't know what has happened, so do not assume the worst. I felt the disturbance,' says Mrs Henders. 'It came to me in my sleep. After so many years, the ties that bind me to that world still pull at me. But I felt no death. Take comfort in that.'

Jake flops back in a chair. It looks like there are tears in his eyes, but maybe it's just the light.

I feel myself starting to adjust, as my brains starts to work again. I realise there are a lot of things I need to say. There's so much I'm feeling, about Jake and me, and suddenly I'm not sure I feel the same way about him anymore. It's not because I now understand how much he's into Cari or my attraction to Archon. No, after everything I've been through, I think I've changed so much that I know Jake and I aren't meant to be together.

I speak to Mrs Henders. 'You knew what was happening to me, didn't you? That's why you said those weird things to me. Why didn't you just tell me?'

'I could sense Shar's hold on you. But, since the snowstorm, I have felt disquiet on every street corner. Until you crossed over and I felt you depart, I didn't know what had occurred.'

I feel sorry for her. I've just escaped from the world that was her home. 'I met Laith,' I say softly.

She draws in a sharp breath. I'd thought she'd want to ask me about him. I would have thought she'd pump me for answers, every minor detail, but she just picks up her own cup of tea from the coffee table and primly takes a sip.

'He told me your story,' I go on. 'But . . . but he went through the *vinarhi.*'

I lean forwards and hold out my hand, the shard clasped tightly. If she touches me while I'm holding the crystal, I can share with her what I know about Laith. 'I've learned some things about working magic. I mean, I made a raft using the Ether to cross back to Earth. When I'm holding this crystal, I can, if you like . . . I can –'

She rears back as if she's scared of touching the crystal. 'No, I don't want it. The memories I have are enough.'

She looks at each of us then, pinning us with her glare.

'We have more important things to think of anyway. I can sense the ripples in the Ether. Something is coming. A great upheaval.'

'They're plotting against us,' I say. 'The Guardians are going to do something against Earth.'

Mrs Henders nods. 'They are jealous and fearful enough to try and sever Shar's ties to every one of the worlds.'

Archon speaks for the first time. 'But Shar, it's the First City and the Last. The axis of the worlds. If they do that . . .'

'Shar will still exist. But the balance will be ripped apart. The other worlds will become unstable. Those most closely linked, such as your own, will be destroyed.'

'We have to stop them! How can we stop them?' Daniel pipes up.

'We can't,' says Archon. 'They're too powerful. This world doesn't stand a chance against them.'

'I wouldn't be so certain,' says Mrs Henders. 'There are ways. But now is not the time for this discussion. It is late, and there are other matters to deal with.'

She looks at me.

'I have to get home,' I say, suddenly jerking out of my stupor. 'Oh my God, Mum will be freaking out. What am I going to tell her?'

'Be calm,' the old woman snaps at me. 'You young people are far too impatient. You forget that time has different meanings in other worlds.'

I look around, hoping to see some proof that what she's saying is true. 'So we've really only been gone a few hours?'

'Yes. Now, I suggest you drink your tea. You will have to convince the people around you that none of this ever happened. Your physical recovery will seem miraculous, and some people will ask questions. As for the crystal shard you carry in your pocket . . . there is power in that piece of Shar and it can be used.'

She looks at me piercingly. 'You are feeling guilty. I can see it in your colours. Why?'

'Because you're offering to help me when I don't deserve it. I . . . I lost it. Your telescope. In the *vinarhi*. It's gone forever.'

'Just as well,' she waves a hand. 'That damn thing has never been anything but trouble.'

I'm relieved and amazed at her reaction. 'If I made something that cool, I'd want to hang onto it. I'd want to keep it forever.'

'There are some things that are worth keeping,' she says. Those hard, deep eyes pass over all of us. Sitting around her lounge room, we must look like a weird group. Jake, sitting on the edge of his chair, thoughtful and worried. Daniel, almost bouncing with excitement. Archon, his sodden robes creating damp patches on the floral couch covering and looking down at his mug as if he's too scared to look anywhere else. And me. Bedraggled, confused and still reeling from everything, 'Usually they're the things you least expect.'

Chapter 30
The Beginning

'I SIMPLY can't explain it,' says Doctor Dracula, shaking her head over the x-ray she's holding. She hasn't stopped shaking her head since I walked in the door with Mum. Yes, walked, with barely a limp. 'There's no sign of scarring, no knitted bone. It's as if there was never any break at all.'

'So, she can play soccer?' Mum asks, glancing at me.

'Well, there's no medical reason to keep her from doing so,' Doctor Dracula admits grudgingly. 'But if she experiences any aches or pains I want you to come back and see me immediately—'

'Thank you, Doctor,' Mum beams at me, and I give her a smile, but it's a thoughtful one.

'I would like to present Keira's case at a conference next month,' Doctor Dracula goes on hurriedly. 'With your permission. It's just such an extraordinary opportunity to further explore this . . . remarkable recovery.'

'No,' I say. I don't shout it, the way I want to, but I've had enough of being treated like a prize specimen. 'No, I don't think that would be a good idea. It might . . . interfere with my schoolwork. I've already missed heaps. You know?'

Mum looks at me, surprised.

'But, Keira,' Doctor Dracula continues in a soothing voice. 'Surely even you are curious as to –'

'No, not really. I can walk and run. That's all I care about.'

Doctor Dracula turns her appealing gaze on Mum, but she's already cutting her off. 'Why don't we just accept that she's healed and move on?'

'But . . . well –' the doctor stutters. 'It's such an interesting case! It's incredible. If we could figure out how this happened, it could help countless others. Don't you understand? This is how science progresses.'

'I've got a friend whose mum used to believe in angels,' I say. 'She never had any proof of it. She just said they were there. Sometimes things just *happen*. Like they're meant to, or something.'

Doctor Dracula is not pleased.

On our way back to the car, Mum glances at me. 'The way you spoke in there,' she says. 'You sounded so . . . different, Keira. You've changed somehow. You've grown up.'

In my pocket is the crystal shard. I pat it briefly, my proof that my trip to Shar actually happened.

Mum doesn't know that I was ever gone. After I crept home from Mrs Henders' house, I found Mum still fast asleep on the lounge. I carefully made my way back into my room and hid my Sharian robes in the back of my closet, along with the crystal shard. I climbed into bed in my old, familiar pyjamas. Mum thinks I spent the night there, resting in preparation for my operation. For a while, she puzzled over what could possibly have happened to my crutches, but thankfully she was too glad about my sudden ability to walk without them to be suspicious.

I feel horrible about not telling her the truth but what else can I do? There are a hundred things I *could* tell her. A thousand things I *want* to tell her. Especially about the things that we're told don't exist. About life; how important it is not to be a blind follower. About dying; how it's possible to want it, to choose it, and not be afraid of it. But most of all, the stuff I learnt about *me*. About *this* world and how I can make a difference in it.

But I can't.

Keeping my voice light, I answer her. 'Bout time, huh?'

She frowns. 'I suppose you'll be able to go back to school. I'll call Mr Alderston about your training –'

'Mum, maybe don't call him just yet.'

'But your ankle is fine.'

'Yeah, it's just . . . I think I want to take a break from it for a bit. I've got some other stuff I want to focus on.'

'Like what?' She sounds worried. I think she just wants everything to go back to normal but it can't. Things are different now. Our world is under threat. At any moment, the Guardians could launch their attack. We don't even know what they'll do, or when it will start.

'Oh, well, Nina has this charity she's organising. She needs some help with it all.'

Mum couldn't be more surprised. 'But soccer –'

'I know it's what I always wanted to do. I just had some time to think these past few days, you know? About people who aren't as lucky as we are. About our whole world. There's so much more we could do . . .'

I think I've lost her, but she's obviously not going to object. 'Of course,' she says.

She turns back to the steering wheel and starts the engine, then hesitates. 'Keira, you're such a capable person. You can do whatever you want with your life and I know you'll do it well. You're strong enough for anything.'

I grin as I catch a whiff of her perfume. Violets. 'Thanks, Mum.'

***

It's late and I can't sleep. I reach under my pillow for the crystal shard. I run my fingers over it, tracing the familiar shape.

I don't get the same dreams about Shar anymore and, even though they scared me, I miss them. They made me feel . . . alive. Now I want to walk in the streets of Shar again. I want to explore the walkways and those towering buildings. I want to see Archon's Etherium and the great library. I want to know more.

I know how Archon felt about our world now. I know why he broke the law, broke the Edict, to study Earth. I know how Cari felt when she was driven to punch a hole through the Ether so she could spy on us. I understand why Mrs Henders allowed herself to be exiled here.

I'm never going to sleep so I push Molly off me and reach for the clothes I left on the floor. 'Come on, girl,' I say. Her eyes light up. Even though I can't tell what she's thinking anymore, I clutch the crystal to see the flickering of colours around her. Excitement. I know how she feels.

I used to do this so often! Almost every night during the summer holidays, I'd sneak down the hallway past Mum's room and out through the front door. From there I'd usually run, Molly keeping up with me easily, and we'd pelt down the street-lit path, past the quiet, sleeping houses. I'd feel my lungs start to burn, just the way they are now, as I cross the Garter Street bridge and cut across the pine plantation that joins Phoenix Park.

He sees me coming. I slip and slide my way down the embankment, as clumsy as ever. Above me, in the boxy dark shape that is the treehouse, he stands up, watching me.

'Hey, Keira,' he says softly.

We've done it up a bit, the treehouse, putting a new tarp over the roof. I've woven some more planks of wood together for the floor, and they're holding strong, just like my raft. It's hardly the Hotel Royale, but it's the best meeting place we've got.

Jake had been the only dubious one. 'It's a cubbyhouse,' he said.

'No, it's not,' Daniel had told him. 'It's Headquarters. Our Base of Operations.'

'Oh, really? For the war we don't even know how to fight?'

I had to admit, I could see his point of view, but it's not in my nature to look on the down side. I've appointed myself Commander in Chief. I'm going to draw up a plan. I'm not just going to fight this war. I'm going to win it.

Leaving Molly sitting faithfully down below, I climb the ladder. I can't see a thing but, going by feel, I manage to climb up to the platform without injury. At the top Archon offers me a hand. I take it and let him pull me up. With the shard in my pocket, I jump as a spark leaps in me, but it's not as overwhelming as it used to be.

I can just make out Archon's smile in the darkness. He's had a haircut, thanks to Nina, who thinks his name is Aaron; Mrs Henders' grandson, whose house was destroyed in the snowstorm and is now living with her for a while.

Nina's all ready to enrol him in our school next week. Of course, all his documents; birth certificate, passport and school records were "lost" in the storm. It'll take a while to get replacements. The school has already taken several kids already on emergency basis. One more won't make a difference.

'You're getting used to it,' Archon says. 'The power of the crystal.'

'I'm getting better at reading it every day,' I say. 'I have to, don't I? If we're going to do anything about this. If we're going to find her . . .' My voice trails off. It still seems impossible. I don't even know where to start.

'You're feeling guilt, Keira. But you can't hold yourself responsible.'

'You don't understand.' I shake my head. 'It's my fault she's out there. My fault she's lost.'

'She knew what she was doing. She asked you to cut the thread, Keira.'

'Yes,' I say. 'But I *wanted* to cut it.'

My voice hitches.

'I hate her, a little bit. More than a bit. I hate that she and Jake . . . and I kind of didn't want her to come back here . . .'

He looks at me and his face is calm. I remember, suddenly, weeks ago, seeing Baz roiling with guilt. What he felt about not going out into the storm to rescue me . . . and how useless it would have been for him to do so. He could have ended up injured as well. Or worse.

He's not touching me, not doing anything with the *ihlwarh*. But I feel the guilt drain out of me anyway. It's stupid to regret the past. I'll just have to do what I can to fix it. I have to find Cari.

'You are very complicated, you humans,' he says. 'I almost think you like to keep secrets and make yourself miserable. Why don't you just tell Jake how much you like him?'

I huff a sigh. 'I don't know. Maybe I will. Probably not, though. All this stuff that's happened –'

'It changes things, doesn't it?' says Archon quietly.

We sit back, and looked up at the sky. All we can see right now are the stars. It's impossible to believe that beyond them is a shining silver city . . . but it's there.

And he's right. Everything is different now.

I reach out and take Archon's hand. Feeling his fingers intertwine with mine, I think it's possible that we can change things, too.

Thank you for reading
ACROSS THE BRIDGE OF ICE.
We hope you enjoyed it.

If you would like to be kept informed of
further releases in the BRIDGES series, or
other new books from Hague Publishing, why
not subscribe to our newsletter at:
www.HaguePublishing.com/subscribe

And if you loved the book and have a
moment to spare we would really
appreciate a short review. Your help in
spreading the word is gratefully received.

About The Author

RUTH Fox is the author of *The Bridges Trilogy* and the award-winning *Monster-boy: Lair of the Grelgoroth*.

She loves to paint, cook and play computer games (very badly). She has a Bachelor of Arts/Diploma of Arts in Professional Writing and Editing. So far she has worked at several far less meaningful or interesting jobs – but writing is her life. She loves science fiction, fantasy, romance, adventure, young adult, adult, literature, old books, new books, and everything in between.

She currently lives with her husband and three very curious and adventurous sons (who also love books) in Ballarat, Victoria.

You can visit her website at: ruth-fox.com, or on Facebook at RuthFoxAuthorandArtist.

Hague

Publishing

www.HaguePublishing.com
PO Box 451 Bassendean
Western Australia 6934